'An absolute triumph. A hymn to mountains, lost children and kind hearts. Tenderly told and fierce in its quest for hope.'
Abi Elphinstone

'A big-hearted story of courage, friendship, refuge and mountains, rich in a sense of place and of nature, and hope for a better world.'
Sunday Times, Books of the Year

'A powerful thread of hope and humanity shines through the story, transforming it into something utterly life-affirming.'
The Observer

'A great story, easy to read, and swiftly devoured.'
Minerva Reads

'Catherine Hyde's black and white illustrations add to the sense of magic that Lauren St John creates in her descriptions of the African and Scottish landscapes… Readers will finish this book more aware of the little things we can do to make the world a better place for everyone.'
BookTrust

'This is a beautiful modern fairy tale of snow, mountains and magic.'
The Week Junior

'Catherine Hyde's beautiful illustrations also add a touch of magic to this tale, helping to transform it into a modern-day fairy-tale that deserves to become a modern-day classic.'
Childtastic Books

'In *The Snow Angel* Lauren St John has created amazing landscapes, peopled by extraordinary characters... Beautifully illustrated by Catherine Hyde, this is a heart-warming story of memory and loss, finding and renewal.'
The School Librarian

'Tender and fierce storytelling, a perfect Christmas read for teens.'
Western Morning News

'A life-affirming and moving story which packs a similar emotional punch to a Michael Morpurgo novel... Compelling and compassionate.'
Books for Keeps

'*The Snow Angel* is uplifting, and a reminder of nature's healing power.'
The Herald

the
SNOW
ANGEL

the
SNOW
ANGEL

LAUREN St JOHN

Illustrated by
CATHERINE HYDE

ZEPHYR

First published in the UK in 2017 by Zephyr,
an imprint of Head of Zeus, Ltd
This paperback edition published in 2018 by Zephyr,
an imprint of Head of Zeus, Ltd

9 7 5 3 1 2 4 6 8

A catalogue record for this book is available from the British Library.

ISBN (PB): 9781786695901
ISBN (E): 9781786695888

Designed by Sue Michniewicz

Printed and bound by CPI Group (UK) Ltd, Croydon, CR0 4YY

Head of Zeus Ltd
First Floor East
5–8 Hardwick Street
London EC1R 4RG
WWW.HEADOFZEUS.COM

CONTENTS

FOR EMELIA & REYHANA,

With love and heartfelt thanks
for all the years of walks, cake,
green mango chutney, support
& wise counsel

'Life is like mountaineering – never look down.'

Sir Edmund Hillary,
mountaineer, explorer
and philanthropist

FRIENDS IN HIGH PLACES

Makena took a deep breath and stepped off the edge of the crevasse.

In the glow of her headlamp, Mount Everest's Khumbu Icefall was a beautiful nightmare: a frozen puzzle of chasms and ice towers. As the sun rose it would melt and shift, becoming more deadly still. The only thing between her and oblivion was a ladder. The first and second rungs held firm. The third wobbled beneath her boot. Terror shot through her but she forced herself on. If Edmund

Hillary and Tenzing Norgay could do it, so could she.

'*Tafadhali!* MAKENA!'

Makena didn't respond. Soon she'd be safe. All she had to do was put one foot in front of the—

'What's up with you, Makena – do you have ants in your pants? How is Gloria expected to make a success of your braids with you wriggling and writhing in the chair?'

Makena looked up from her book, eyes glazed, heart racing.

Modern-day Nairobi sharpened into focus. She returned to reality with a bump, the silent snowfields of her imagination giving way to the yellow heat of Kenya's dry season and the blast of dryers and Beyoncé. Her mother was leaning round the door of Blessings Hair & Beauty, her expression both exasperated and tender.

Makena grinned. 'Sorry, Mama, I was in a good bit.'

Gloria tugged hard on a braid to get Makena's attention.

'Ouch!'

'Any more nonsense and I'll take out my clippers and give you a buzz cut,' the hairdresser warned.

'That's fine by me,' Makena said cheerfully. 'Baba has a buzz cut and it's great. It feels like moss. He says it's very practical for climbing mountains.'

Her mother laughed. 'Yes, but luckily all you have to worry about is getting to and from school. Do me a favour and try the braids for a few months. They suit you. If you're not happy, Gloria can shave an image of Mount Everest on the side of your head. I won't care.'

Makena almost jumped out of her chair. 'Cool!'

Gloria snatched up her clippers, switching them on for added effect. Makena shrank into her chair.

Her mother rolled her eyes. 'I'm joking, Makena. Now sit still. You're almost done.'

'But we've been here for three solid hours,' sulked Makena. She glowered round at the packed salon, raised to sauna temperature by the press of women who came to Blessings as much for the quality of the gossip as the weaves. 'All this time I could have been practising climbing or reading a book on abseiling. Real mountaineers don't care about their hair.'

'Yes, and it shows,' her mother retorted. 'Some of those people are only one step from the cave.'

'Looks don't matter when you're climbing the Ice Window route and watching out for avalanches. Baba says the only thing that counts when he's guiding clients up Mount Kenya is keeping his head when everyone else is losing theirs. And, of course, willpower and good lungs. That's what I'll be thinking about the day after tomorrow.'

Makena snapped shut her book and bounced in

her seat. 'Oh, Mama, I cannot wait. I'm afraid I might die of excitement before we ever get there.'

'I give up!' Gloria whipped the towel from Makena's shoulders. 'They don't pay me enough for this. You can go as you are with your hair sticking up. If anyone asks what went wrong, tell them you were mowed down by an avalanche. This is the result. Don't you dare mention Blessings Hair & Beauty. We will be ruined.'

Makena waited on the steps of the salon as her mother paid, adding a large tip to soothe Gloria's nerves. The January sun was slow-cooking Kenyatta street market. Sweating customers haggled over cassava, tomatoes and barrels of smoking corn. Chickens protested from a basket on the back of a bicycle. A trader chased a goat intent on gobbling all his spinach.

On the road beyond, battered cars, listing buses

and rickshaws struggled by like a ramshackle circus. Their hooting and braying assaulted Makena's eardrums. Nairobi traffic was infamous. Not long ago there'd been an eleven-hour jam.

Gloria's teenage daughter joined her in what passed for shade beneath the salon awning. Nadira smiled and her lips moved.

'Excuse me?' Makena was back on Everest with Hillary and Sherpa Tenzing in 1953. She returned to the present only reluctantly.

'I said I liked what you were saying in there, about climbing. How you defended it and were so passionate about it. You make it sound as if the mountains are your friends.'

Makena's mother emerged from the salon, stuffing her purse into her bag. 'Let's go before Gloria changes her mind and comes after you with the clippers.'

As they dodged commuters and bicycles on the

rush-hour streets, Makena couldn't stop thinking about what Nadira had said. Without knowing it, she'd summed up something Makena had felt her whole life but had never been able to put into words.

The mountains were her friends.

BAD FAIRIES

akena had been born and raised in the city and yet whenever she left it to go to Nanyuki, an elephant climbed off her chest.

It wasn't a real one (obviously) and only very tiny (an elephant's toenail, perhaps), but in Nairobi it was always there. The traffic was so snarled up and everyone was so squashed up that Makena frequently felt as if she was being flattened one molecule at a time by an unseen force. She was familiar with molecules because her mother was a science teacher and Makena knew off by heart that a molecule was a group of atoms bonded together and an atom was the smallest particle of a chemical element in existence.

As Nairobi's gap-toothed skyline shrank behind Mr Chivero's Land Cruiser, Makena breathed easier. The road ahead was ruler-straight. Concrete and crowds gave way to lush plantations of coffee, tea and bananas. Beneath a dizzying blue sky, roadside vendors beamed behind colourful pyramids of pineapples, tangerines and avocados.

Makena squinted at the horizon, stretching her seat belt to its limit. She wanted to be the first to see the ripple of mauve that would hint at a distant Mount Kenya.

In the front seat, Mr Chivero slurped noisily from a plastic cup and sighed with satisfaction. 'Kenyan AA coffee and condensed milk – the driver's best friend. Two mugs of this could jump-start a car with a flat battery.'

'Can I try some, Uncle Samson?' asked Makena, eyeing the treacly brew. Mr Chivero was a Zimbabwean colleague of her father, Kagendo Wambora, at New Equator Tours. He was not a relation, but in keeping with local tradition she respectfully addressed friends of her parents as aunt or uncle.

'*Please,*' said her mother.

'Please, Uncle Samson...'

'Check with your mama.'

Betty sloshed a little into the lid of the flask, blew on it to cool it and passed it between the seats to her daughter. One swallow of its smoky-sweetness and Makena's eyeballs almost exploded.

Mr Chivero let out a delighted cackle. 'Eh heh! What did I tell you? It has a kick like a giraffe. Too strong for children, but perfect for me. I myself shall never have to worry about sleeping at the wheel and winding up in a ditch like that unfortunate taxi.'

He tapped his window. They were passing the rusting wreck of a Matatu Madness cab, so nicknamed because many of their drivers were speed-merchants and vagabonds. The way the minivan's ribs curved out of the long grass reminded Makena of a dinosaur she'd once seen in the museum. She shivered. Were the occupants of the taxi now extinct like the Allosaurus?

'Beware of too much caffeine, Mr Chivero,' cautioned Makena's mother, taking the cup from her daughter's unresisting hands. 'It is not good for your health.'

There was a snort. 'Better a hundred litres of coffee than to rely on a Tokoloshe to take the wheel, as some lorry drivers do in my home country, Zimbabwe.'

Makena leaned forward. 'What's a Tokoloshe, Uncle Samson?'

'Some say that, in the beginning, it was a friendly

fairy who loved children. But for many years now it has been nothing but a mean and mischievous water-sprite.'

'Does it still have wings?'

'It does not, but that's all anyone knows for sure. One man will tell you that the Tokoloshe who wrecked his house was a wrinkly dwarf with porcupine hair. Others swear that when Night throws his cloak over Zimbabwe the Tokoloshe becomes a baboon with eyes like cooking fires. Those are the ones most popular with long-distance lorry drivers. When the driver wants to sleep, he lies down and lets the Tokoloshe take over.'

Makena giggled. 'You're making up stories.'

Mr Chivero did not laugh with her. 'In my country, there are villages where every bed is built on bricks because the Tokoloshe is afraid of heights. When I am in Zimbabwe, that is the only bed I will sleep in. But lorry drivers who make a deal with one cannot escape so easily. If they think they can bribe the creature with beer or sweets, they are mistaken. Once you are in league with the Tokoloshe, it is insatiable.'

'What's insatiable?'

'It's what you are, Miss Makena, once you open a box of chocolates. You want more, more, more.'

'Tradition is important but don't fill the child's head with superstition, Samson Chivero,' chided Makena's mother. 'You know very well that there is no such thing as the Tokoloshe. It's a myth. These goblins are the favourite excuse of lazy drivers, untidy teenagers and husbands who have drunk too much or gambled away the family grocery money.'

Mr Chivero overtook a donkey cart. Makena twisted round to catch a glimpse of the animals' patient, dark eyes. Their ears flopped like the leaves of an umbrella tree after a storm.

'Shamwari,' he said, using the Shona word, 'I admit you have a point – some shirkers and bad husbands use the tales of the Tokoloshe for their own wicked ends. But even you, a modern woman of science, know that some things cannot be explained.'

'I know nothing of the kind. I choose to put my trust in the scientific method. Everything can be explained by physics in the end and if it can't be explained it's not the end.'

'What about Lucas, your childhood friend – the one who lived among the fishes? What does physics have to say about him?'

Makena's mother went stiff. For a long moment no one spoke. The silence was so thick you could have eaten it with bread and butter.

The suspense was too much for Makena. 'Who's Lucas, Mama?'

'Someone I knew before you were born, my dear. So long ago, I can barely remember him. The only other person who knew his tale is your father. It seems he unwisely shared it with Samson.'

Samson protested and Makena begged to be let in on the secret, but her mother refused to budge.

She pointed ahead. 'Makena, look!'

In the distance was a smudge of powder-blue with a fluffy mawingu (cloud) on top. A sort of mountain cake. Makena had spent hundreds of hours dreaming about great mountains of the world though, for her, none had the pull of Mount Kenya. She could feel it now, calling to her.

Her heart corkscrewed in her chest, straining to be free.

But the mountain was still some way off and she was dying to hear about Lucas who had lived among the fishes, the more so because her mother was set on evading the subject. Nobody could live underwater. What could Uncle Samson mean?

Before she could press her mama further, something unexpected happened.

'Take the next turning on the right, Mr Chivero,' instructed her mother. 'I have a surprise for Makena – a special visit to Tambuzi Rose Farm.'

Makena's face fell. Surprises were wonderful and a rose farm did sound fun, but the mountain was waiting. Her mama caught her expression before she could rearrange it.

She smiled. 'You're always in such a hurry, Makena. The mountain is not going anywhere. If all you do is run, run, run, you can miss what is right in front of you.'

HOW TO ESCAPE FROM
A BUFFALO

akena took a sip of mango juice and relaxed against a rhino. No real, red-blooded rhino would have put up with a girl using it for shade. However, this one was made of wood and, as such, was indifferent. It gazed serenely over Nanyuki Civil Airstrip, gateway to Mount Kenya, from the lawn of Barney's Restaurant.

The focus of Makena's attention was her father. He was on the runway, seeing off a group of bearded, grizzly-sized Canadians. From a distance, he looked slight by comparison. In reality, his tight, lithe frame was as hard as the volcanic rocks on the mountain he loved.

Once the tourists were aboard the eight-seater Cessna, he assisted in the loading of their luggage. His movements were sleepy but somehow sleekly efficient. Rarely could he be made to hurry, but his daughter and clients knew that in the event of an emergency he'd be a blur of well-oiled action, like a revolver only ever used once.

He watched the plane lurch into the blue with a tractor roar before coming over. Makena ran to greet him and he whirled her round.

'Ready for your first attempt at climbing the mountain, Makena? Are you strong like a lion?'

She giggled. 'No, Baba. Strong like Tenzing Norgay.'

'That strong? Hmmn, I'll need to keep my eye on you. Next you'll be after my job.'

'How has this happened?' cried his wife, giving him a hug. 'How have I ended up with two mountain goats?'

'Just lucky, I guess,' Makena piped up.

'Is that right? Well, can you keep some luck for yourself? I want the two of you home safe and sound.'

'I thought you didn't believe in luck? It isn't scientific.'

Her mother laughed. 'That's true. I don't. But I do believe in miracles. I got you, didn't I?'

The mountain was no longer a smudge on the horizon. It filled the windscreen. Makena tingled with adrenaline and awe. She couldn't decide whether to leap out of the 4x4 and plant her second-hand hiking boots on Mount Kenya's volcanic rocks, or run away in case she wasn't the bold and gifted climber of her dreams.

An hour or so earlier they'd exchanged the tarred road for rough dirt. Now they followed the winding track through the rainforest. Mint-fresh air patterned Makena's arms with goose-bumps.

It was early afternoon but already there was a bite to the breeze. The mountain's plunging overnight temperatures often caught tourists off guard. 'But it's Africa!' they'd croak as they were stretchered away with hypothermia. 'Mount Kenya straddles the Equator!'

'Look at Batian,' her father would tell his clients, indicating the highest of the mountain's three peaks. 'What do you see up there? Those white patches — they're not decorations. Whether you're on Everest or Mount Kenya, snow falls when ice crystals stick together in clouds and the temperature is lower than two degrees Celsius. There's not one temperature for snow in Nepal and another in Kenya.'

After his last technical climb — those were ones where he led experienced mountaineers on ice and rock climbs up Batian and Nelion — he'd brought Makena a jar of snow from the Lewis Glacier. She'd been fascinated by snow since she was tiny. It wasn't snow when it reached her; the African heat had seen to that. It was just an old jam jar filled with water. But Makena knew it had been *born* snow, at over five thousand metres. To her, that was all that mattered.

The snow jar was one of her most treasured possessions. It sat on her bedside table alongside a posy of pressed wildflowers, an eggcup filled with volcanic ash and driftwood in the shape of a pouncing leopard.

Like the climbing wall he'd built at the back of their home, they were supposed to make up for her father's long absences. But it was a trade-off for him as much as her. That's why he'd made Makena a promise.

Next time he had a break, he'd take her on her first ever mountain adventure.

'Just you and me, Baba?'

'Just us.'

Now at last they were on their way. Makena felt strangely shy. She was glad that her father did most of the talking. As he drove, he pointed out landmarks. Here's where he'd gathered honey and chopped firewood to support his single mother and half-brother and pay for his primary school education. Here's where he'd been struck by a flaming branch while fighting wildfires as a teenage volunteer.

'That was the first time the mountain thanked me.'

'How could it do that, Baba?'

'Because, Makena, that is nature's way. She's like your mama. She might tell you off or punish you for doing wrong or being careless, but she also gives you the tools to make everything better.'

He rolled up his shirtsleeve and showed her a lightning bolt scar above his elbow. It was a fraction of a shade lighter than the cocoa dark surrounding it. 'See that? Practically invisible. Fixed it myself with mountain honey and aloe vera. Best burn treatment in the world.'

They wound upwards through the mountain's rings of vegetation. First came luxuriant forests of cedar, camphor and wild olive, their branches snarled with vines. Some bits had been decimated by loggers and those made Makena's chest hurt, as if each missing tree had taken a piece of her. The mountain tribes farmed here too, their crops creeping higher and wider with each passing year.

To each, Mount Kenya was sacred. The Embu called it *Kirenia*, Mountain of Whiteness, and thought of it as the Home of God. Many built their houses with front doors facing it.

Tall, mahogany-limbed Maasai, wrapped in red *Shúkà*, grazed their cattle on the northern slopes. Gazing up from the triangle of shadow Mount Kenya cast on the surrounding plains, it appeared to them as *Ol Donyo Keri*, Mountain of Stripes.

But none were as connected to the mountain as the Kikuyu and the Embu, her father's tribe. For both, it was a spiritual home. In Embu and Gĩkũyũ tradition, *Ngai*, the Supreme Being and giver of life force, lived on the mountain after coming down from the sky. The Kikuyu called Mount Kenya *Kĩrĩ Nyaga*, God's Resting Place. Its snow-capped peaks were *Ngai's* crown.

Looked at in that way, Makenà thought, the jar on her bedside table did not simply contain melted snow. It held a sliver of God's crown.

Onwards and upwards they went. Makena had yearned for this day for so long she could hardly believe it was here. Face pressed to the cold window, she watched thickets of cloud-dusting mountain bamboo go by. In places it was ten metres tall, its yellow culms so densely packed they choked off nearly all light and sound. If a bird or ill wind set the bamboo whispering it could, her father told her, chill the blood of a grown man.

When the road ended, they parked. Makena clambered out stiffly. For the first time since she'd left Nairobi, she was able to properly fill her lungs. The pure, cool air gave her a head rush. Adrenaline revived her. She'd worried that the reality of the mountain might not match her vivid imaginings, but its ancient energy surged through her soles like an electric charge.

They'd stopped for supplies at a supermarket in Nanyuki and her backpack felt as if it was filled with rocks. Makena was glad. It tethered her to the earth. In her current state of bliss, she was in danger of floating up to the Lewis Glacier.

Her father put a steadying hand on her shoulder. 'Makena, it's possible that we will encounter elephant and buffalo as we walk through the forest. Do you remember what I taught you? What is the first rule about meeting an elephant in the wild?'

'The elephant always has right of way.'

'Correct. The same applies to buffalo, zebras, snakes and leopards. Unfortunately, the buffalo is a very hot-tempered animal. Even if you give him right of way, he will sometimes get road rage and attack. What do you do if this happens?'

'I must throw down my backpack and lie on the ground,' said Makena, trying to convince herself that if a crazed, two-tonne buffalo were thundering towards her, she'd lie down in its path.

'And why is that?'

'Because the Maasai say that if you're flat like bread, a buffalo can't gore you or toss you because of the shape of their horns… Are you *sure* this is true, Baba? Has anyone ever tried it and survived? Wouldn't the buffalo just crush you with its hard head instead? Maybe it would be better if I climbed a tree. I'm extremely good at climbing trees.'

'You are the best tree climber in Kenya, no doubt about it. If there is a tree in sight, I'd recommend that you get on up. But a good mountaineer always has a Plan B. Say a buffalo catches you in the open, where there is not so much as a blade of grass. What would you do then?'

'Oh. *Ohhhh*. Okay, I'll lie flat.'

He grinned. 'Good girl. Now are you ready for the mountain, Makena?'

'Ready, Baba.'

SIGNS

akena awoke terrified, with no idea where she was. She came crawling up from the dank, dark swamp of a nightmare and surfaced blind, damp with sweat. Her cheeks were wet too, as if she'd been crying.

For a minute that felt like a year, she could see and hear nothing. Gradually, mercifully, sounds and shapes made themselves known: the music of the nearby river, the curve of the tent-flap open to the stars, and her father in his sleeping bag beside her.

She shook his arm urgently. There was no response. She shook him again. Nothing. Holding her own breath, she waited for him to inhale. He didn't. She breathed twice more and still he was motionless.

He was dead! Her baba was dead and she was alone in the wilderness, easy picking for hungry wild animals.

Makena grabbed his hand. 'Baba, don't leave me,' she half-sobbed.

His eyes opened a fraction. 'Don't be afraid, Makena girl,' he mumbled. 'The hyenas won't hurt you while I'm here. They're not as fierce as they look.'

Then he was gone again, snoring faintly.

It was enough. Makena lay back down, reassured. Her pulse rate slowed. She told herself off for being so silly. So childish. Hadn't her mama said that nightmares were simply brain soup? Fears, ideas and memories all mushed up together.

The horror of the dream was not easily dismissed. The details had slithered away, slippery as a mamba, but the black, suffocating venom of it throbbed in Makena's veins.

She fixed her gaze on the comforting triangle of night sky. Before turning in, her father had tied back the tent-flap so Makena could lie in her sleeping bag and see stars sprinkled like sherbet above the black crags.

Strange that she should suffer bad dreams after one of the best days of her life. She blamed the hyenas. Their laughter had unsettled her. There'd been nothing funny about it. One minute she'd been enjoying a peaceful dinner by the campfire; the next it was as if the dead were being raised.

The first primal, ghostly whoop had sent her scuttling to her father's side. He'd hugged her tight and told her the hyenas wouldn't hurt her while he was with her. '*They're not as fierce as they look.*'

It worked until an unseen cackle of hyenas joined the chorus. Their deranged howls and coughs ricocheted round the gorge. Spooked, the fat, fluffy tree hyraxes responded with equally chilling screams. Makena saw red eyes and hunch-shouldered silhouettes lurking in every shifting shadow.

'Should we hide in the tent, Baba? What if they gang up on us, like wolves?'

Her father laughed but not unkindly. He was making her a bush hot water bottle — a brick-sized rock heated by the fire and wrapped in hessian.

'No, Makena, they will not be coming for our fresh curried trout and rice. They're too busy squabbling over their own dinner — probably something rotten. They prefer carcasses when they smell more ... interesting.'

Makena was not convinced. She'd heard too many stories about hyenas using their immense jaws to snap off people's arms as if they were twigs.

'These Mount Kenya hyenas are clever,' her father continued. 'They know the Swahili proverb: "A cowardly hyena lives for many years". It's one that works for people too.'

'But it's bad to be a coward, Baba. If you're a coward it means you're weak and pitiful and can't be trusted.'

His eyes twinkled. 'I can see you've given the matter some serious thought. As you get older, you will discover that life's not so simple. There are times when it's wise to be cautious and avoid too many risks, especially if you have a family and want to be around for years to take care of them.'

'Like you?'

'Yes, like me.'

'But you're brave, Baba. You wouldn't be a climber if you were not. If being cowardly is sometimes a smart thing, does that mean being brave is sometimes a stupid thing?'

He laughed. 'It's too late at night for trick questions. All I know is this. If you are brave for a noble cause, because you want to help others or fight for justice or save a life – perhaps even your *own* life – then being brave is the best thing of all. Now this chattering is making me thirsty. Are you going to help me make some *chai* or do I have to do it on my own?'

Makena tossed and turned in her sleeping bag. There wasn't a whole lot of sleeping going on. Her mind teemed with images. If she heard a noise outside, she tried to persuade herself that it was a rock hyrax looking for scraps, not a hyena on the look-out for a crunchy and delicious child. She reminded herself that, so far, the mountain had proved itself a friend.

On their walk through the mossy glades of the cloud forest that afternoon, she and her father had not been threatened by marauding buffalo or elephants. Far from it. The largest creatures they'd clapped eyes on were a troop of colobus monkeys and a dainty, black-fronted duiker.

At this altitude, the trees were mostly short, their branches twisted and plastered with lichen. The only evidence that elephants ever passed between them was a lone footprint. Makena had bent to examine the faint, lacy sketch of it. Her own boot prints were twice as deep.

'But where are the others? I mean, it can't be a one-legged elephant.'

'They're there if you know how to look for them, but you might need a microscope,' her father told her.

45

'Africa's giants are light on their feet. There are Mount Kenya mole shrews who leave deeper tracks.'

He showed her the place where he'd broken his ankle just hours into his first ever job as a mountain porter.

'If I'd been doing something daring it wouldn't have been so painful, but I just tripped over a tussock of elephant grass and landed badly. The other porters nearly died laughing. I nearly died of embarrassment.'

Mobile phones had not yet been invented and two-way radios were never much use on the mountain. The expedition clients, wealthy businessmen, had been keen to proceed, and no guide or porter could be spared to help Baba. He'd been forced to hop, crawl and drag himself down the mountain to a point where he could wait for help. The only thing that had kept his spirits up was the tea he brewed from the yellow flowers of St John's Wort.

Makena had heard this story many times but seeing where it happened made it more real.

'How come you didn't just give up and choose an easier job? Lion taming or something. That's what I would do if I broke my ankle on my first time up the mountain. I'd think it was a sign.'

'A sign? A sign of what? That I was too clumsy or stupid to be a mountain guide and must give up on my dreams? No, Makena, climbing is like the journey of life. You start slowly. You try one way and if it doesn't work out or you meet some obstacles, you keep searching until you find another trail. There is always a second chance. If you keep on walking and keep on trying, you'll get there in the end.'

A CLOSE ENCOUNTER

'Are you sure you're okay, Makena?' her father asked for the third time. 'You have been waiting for this day for so many years, I predicted I'd have to restrain you from flying up the mountain like a helium balloon. Instead you are quiet. Were you able to sleep? Did you wake me last night because you were afraid of the hyenas or did I dream that?'

'You dreamed it, Baba,' lied Makena. 'If I was restless it was because I was a little cold.'

'A little? Then you are stronger than I am. The

night frosts are vicious. A famous professor by the name of Hedberg once said that on equatorial mountains such as Mount Kenya it can be "summer every day and winter every night". Hopefully, your bush hot water bottle kept you warm.'

'It helped so much. Sorry if I'm not talking, Baba. I'm trying to take everything in so I never forget it.'

That part was true. The steep, muddy descent to the River Kathita was already lodged in her memory. In the arc of her father's headlamp, the ripples and eddies had been as black-gold as an oil slick. The current had sucked at her legs. Stepping from rock to slimy rock in five a.m. darkness had been heart-stopping too, but in a good way. It was the kind of adventure she'd always longed for.

At first light they'd passed the Rutundu Log Cabins where Prince William had proposed to Kate Middleton. Makena tried telling herself that nothing evil could happen in a place where future princesses accepted marriage proposals, but the sense of foreboding that had gripped her since her nightmare clung to her like a snakeskin.

She was tempted to feign an injury and end their expedition right there. What if the dream had been a premonition? But her father had chosen that moment to turn to her with a smile.

'I'm so glad you are here with me, daughter. I've waited eleven years to share my mountain with you. I thought this day would never come.'

Feeling guilty, Makena looped her arm through his and walked with more enthusiasm up the rocky trail.

As the sun rose, it revealed a moorland landscape of staggering beauty. Apple-green *Erica*, taller than Makena and speckled with tiny pink flowers, carpeted the slopes. A Verreaux's eagle, the most regal hunter in all of Kenya, wheeled overhead.

Watching the black eagle calmed Makena. She tried to keep it in sight. Her father crunched along the path beside her. 'My Scottish clients tell me that the moors and tarns on Mount Kenya remind them of the Highlands and lakes in their own country. They don't call them lakes, though. Their word is "loch".'

All Makena knew about Scotland was that the men wore tartan skirts and everyone ate haggis, which her mother had explained was a combination of cow's stomach lining stuffed with sheep's heart, liver and lungs and oatmeal, a much-loved national dish. Makena, a vegetarian, had been in no hurry to visit the country.

Now she revised her opinion. If the Scottish Highlands were anything like this, they must be close to heaven.

At Lake Rutundu, a rowing boat was waiting for them. Makena clutched at its sides as her father pushed off from the shore. The wooden seat felt chilly beneath her trousers. Jurassic trout glided through the clear shallows beneath the boat's peeling hull.

Breakfast was peanut butter and jam sandwiches, a bruised banana and a flask of *chai* out on the water. The lake was so still the boat barely shivered beneath them. They bobbed in the reflection of the mountain, an extinct stratovolcano that was over three million years old.

Her father was in his element. 'My ambition is to have a view like this when me and your mama retire. I'm not in love with cities. I have no wish to become a millionaire. I want to grow old looking out at mountains and water.'

Makena dropped her crusts overboard. A quicksilver shoal shot up to snatch the crumbs.

'Which is the best mountain, Baba – Kilimanjaro or Mount Kenya?' She knew the answer but never tired of hearing it.

He scoffed. 'Kili is a giant hill, easy for mzungu tourists. Mount Kenya is a real mountain.'

'But Kilimanjaro is the highest in Africa. It's close to six thousand metres. Mount Kenya is only five thousand one hundred and ninety-nine metres.'

'Yes, but before it erupted Mount Kenya's original crater was a thousand metres higher, making it the highest in Africa.'

Using her sleeping bag as a pillow, Makena lay back and mentally mapped the route they'd be taking to Lake Alice. It was a tough but straightforward hike via Rutundu Hill. What could go wrong? What was it that her intuition was trying to warn her of?

'Do you ever get scared when you're on the mountain, Baba? Have you ever been afraid of dying?'

'Once. I was climbing the Diamond Couloir, an icy gully that splits the Southwest face. You start with eight metres of overhanging rock, dry-tooling. Dry-tooling is—'

'—When you climb a rock face with an ice axe and using crampons or rock shoes,' finished Makena.

He laughed. 'I always forget – you are already a mountaineer in theory. All you need is some practice. So anyway, I got through the hard part – the overhanging section – easy enough. But halfway up the couloir, a chunk of ice calved. That's what they call it when seracs fracture: calving. I felt the draught of its passing. If I hadn't shaved, the serac would have done it for me. *Hakuna Matata.* No worries. I am here to tell the tale.'

'You could have died, Baba!'

'But I didn't. Instinct told me that all was not well on the mountain that day. I was on the look-out for disaster and I was ready for it. Each climber has his or her rules of mountaineering and those must become second nature. Ignoring them, forgetting them, can cost you your life.'

'What are your rules, Baba?'

'You know them better than I do, Makena.'

Still he ticked them off on his fingers. 'Always triple-check the weather and your clothing and equipment before setting out to climb even the easiest or most familiar route. Do all you can to minimise risk. Keep the pace of the slowest person in your group. Listen to your body and your mind. For me, that's number one. *Trust your intuition.*'

Infected with some unspecified terror, his daughter stayed silent beside him.

They moored on the far side of the lake. Her father took out his fishing rod. Makena set off to explore the shore. Lilies, herbs and blue delphinium lined the path. Proteas with velvety yellow flowers brushed her hands.

Birds sang and flitted. The alpine chats were so tame they barely moved out of her way. Jewelled sunbirds drank nectar from the gladioli. Red-winged starlings hunted through the lobella for snails.

It was every bit the mountain paradise Makena had imagined. She only wished that she felt better so she could enjoy it more. In a little while, she and her father would begin their two-hour hike up to Lake Alice and Ithangune Ridge. She'd waited for this day for so long. It seemed unfair that it had been tainted.

Through the reeds, she glimpsed a narrow beach. She wandered down and kneeled on the fine sand. Cupping her hands, she washed her face in the freezing tarn. It made her feel alive. She smiled at her own reflection.

A rustle of reeds set her pulse racing. The sunlight on the water cast dazzling shards of light. Through wet lashes, Makena saw a dark gold shape emerge from the greenery. A duck? A mongoose?

Reluctant to move in case she scared it, Makena became a statue. She tried not to breathe. The creature dipped its head and drank.

Makena blinked rapidly and her vision cleared. It was a bat-eared fox, backlit by the sparkling lake. There was no mistaking its bushy tail or the curving black ears that cupped its elfin, pointed face. Its golden brown fur was silky-soft. Makena was tempted to reach out and stroke it.

The fox lifted its head and turned a fearless gaze on her. There were diamond droplets in its whiskers.

'Are you there, Makena?' Baba came trampling through the reeds. 'We'd better go if we want to reach Lake Alice before the Gates of Mist come down between Batian and Nelion.'

The fox fled and took the shadows with it. The most intense happiness Makena had ever known flooded through her.

'Baba, Baba!' She raced up the bank. 'You won't believe it. I saw a bat-eared fox. He was so close I could almost touch him. He was magical. Completely magical.'

'A fox by the lake? I'm not so sure, Makena. I've never heard of any on the mountain. They tend to live on the plains, in dens with their families. Maybe it was a silver-backed jackal. They can look similar from a distance. Or perhaps a white-tailed mongoose.'

For a second Makena was thrown. Could it have been a jackal? But, no, she was positive. The shining fox had stared right at her. It had banished the gloom and given her back her joy.

'It was a bat-eared fox with water diamonds in its whiskers. I'm a hundred per cent certain.'

He put his arm across her shoulders. 'A bat-eared fox with water diamonds in its whiskers? If you say you saw it, that's good enough for me. Seeing is believing, Makena. Seeing is believing.'

THE DOOMSDAY GERM

'We'll be back in a week. You won't have time to miss us.'

Makena's mother bent to enfold her in butter-soft arms. She smelled of Ponds Cold Cream and love. 'Be good and do your best with your school essay. You have plenty to talk about after your Mount Kenya adventure. Neat handwriting, please — not that kind you do when you're in a hurry so it looks as if a drunken ant has performed a gymnastics routine on the page. And no reading books with a torch after lights out.'

Makena helped her zip up her old suitcase. There was a tear in one side, patched with duct tape. She missed her mama and baba already, but it seemed selfish to say so when they were only going because they wanted to help her sick Aunt Mary. In her entire life Makena had not spent a single night apart from at least one of her parents. At her school, where the majority of children had lone parents, divorced parents or no parents, that made her a rarity.

Her father came into the bedroom, tapping his watch. 'What's taking so long, Betty? Samson says we will miss the flight. This Nairobi traffic, it's too terrible. We only have an hour to get to the airport and it can easily take three.'

'*Haraka, haraka, haina baraka,*' his wife teased him in Swahili. 'Hurry, hurry has no blessings. Isn't that what you're always telling me, Kagendo?'

He laughed. 'On an ordinary day, that's my philosophy. But there will be no blessings if we miss the plane either. Your sister needs us. Makena and I will take your suitcase to the car. Check that you have our passports and tickets to Sierra Leone.'

Whenever Makena thought about the West African country where her Aunt Mary lived which, if she were truthful, wasn't often, she pictured rushing coffee-coloured rivers in which diamonds floated like glittering fish. During the long civil war, children her own age and younger had been torn from their families, given automatic weapons and sent into the jungles to fight over the precious gems.

These 'blood' diamonds were later sold to rich people in far-flung places where, ironically, they symbolised romance and eternal love. Some women wore blood diamond rings their whole lives without ever pausing to think of the empty-eyed children who'd scrabbled, fought and died in the mud for them.

The war had ended in 2002. For the past six years Freetown, Sierra Leone's capital, had been home to Betty's sister Mary, an aid worker with a charity that provided villages with clean drinking water.

At least, that's what she normally did. A week ago, she'd fallen ill with malaria in a remote rural area. There'd been problems getting her to a doctor and now the situation was grave. Makena's father had been granted emergency leave by New Equator Tours and a substitute teacher was going to take her mother's classes. Their plan was to find Aunt Mary the best treatment they could afford in Sierra Leone then bring her back to Kenya to recover.

Makena was struggling to take in the sudden turn of events. Two days ago she'd been on top of the world. Well, not the top, perhaps, but certainly on the second or third storey of *Ngai's* mountain home. She'd stood on Ithangune Ridge and planted a flag made from a stick and a crumpled red T-shirt.

It was more usual for mountaineers to erect a flag when they reached a summit but even Point Lenana, Mount Kenya's most reachable summit, required acclimatisation and a five-day round-trip — not something that was possible for Makena.

'Next time,' her father had promised.

It didn't matter. Makena was content. On the hike to Lake Alice, she'd had a Verreaux's eagle's view of the Great Rift Valley, its plains speckled with zebra, wildebeest and giraffe. She'd seen the gleaming white peaks of Batian and Nelion and had a close encounter with a fox.

The idyll had ended as soon as they came down the mountain and the first urgent message pinged on her father's phone. To avoid altitude sickness, they'd had no choice but to spend a night in Nanyuki before speeding to Nairobi early next morning.

And now Baba was leading Makena out on to the street, suitcase in hand. Her rucksack bulged with the clothes and books she'd need for the next seven days.

'It's really six and a half,' her mother had pointed out. 'Not even a week.'

After stowing the case in Uncle Samson's vehicle, her father took a photo from his pocket. It showed him clinging to a wall of ice by his fingertips. He wore a huge grin.

'A client sent this to me. You can keep it. Don't show your mama. It'll make her nervous.'

'Yes, you'd better not show her or else she'll make you take up accountancy instead,' retorted his wife, overhearing.

'You wouldn't,' accused Makena. 'You like it that he's heroic.'

Her mother laughed. 'I shouldn't admit it but, yes, I do.'

'You are cutting it fine to get to the airport,' grumbled Mr Chivero. 'If I could drive like Lewis Hamilton, that would be one thing, but Nairobi is so gridlocked it is not possible to exceed the pace of a bicycle with a flat tyre. Not unless you are a Matatu Madness taxi. Then anything is possible. If someone gets in your way, you just ramp over the top of them like 007 in a Bond movie.'

'Relax, dear man, Makena's lift will be here at any moment and we will go. Makena, did you pack your toothbrush?'

'No, Mama, I'm going to use twigs and leaves.'

'Don't be smart.'

'Sorry, but don't worry so much.'

'That's what mothers do. We worry.'

A car pulled up. Out stepped her mother's

colleague, Shani. She was a Kenyan maths teacher married to a Chinese man who had a computer business. They had four children — a baby, a toddler, and super-bright eleven-year-old twins, Li and Leo. They were the busiest family Makena knew. Every spare hour was devoted to running back and forth from Wing Chung lessons to Mandarin and piano. However, they were also very nice, and Li and Makena had a love of reading in common.

'Give my best to your sister,' Shani told Betty. 'I hope she makes a speedy recovery. You're sure it's malaria she has and not the Doomsday Germ? That's what they were calling it on the news this morning.'

'What's the Doomsday Germ?' asked Makena.

Her mother gave her a squeeze. She was annoyed with Shani for mentioning it, Makena could tell. 'If you are talking about the Ebola virus, Shani, then, no, Mary does not have that. She's been diagnosed with malaria. There is a small Ebola outbreak on the border with Guinea, but it's been contained. We will be many hundreds of miles from there, near Kenema. As soon as my sister is well enough to travel, we'll return to Nairobi – possibly even sooner than Sunday.'

Her husband came over. 'Betty, we must go.'

He gave Makena's braids an affectionate tug. 'See you later, alligator.'

'In a while, crocodile.'

'*Nakupenda!* Love you,' her mother said, cupping Makena's face with her palms and kissing the tip of her nose.

'Love you too. Give a big hug to Aunt Mary. I'll say prayers.'

Shani opened the car door and Makena squeezed in beside the twins.

'Hey, see what I've got.' Li thrust a mystery novel into her hands. 'It's the latest one in the series.'

As Shani put the car into gear and moved off down the road, Makena was absorbed in reading the blurb on the cover of the book. That's the thing that haunted her afterwards. She never looked back.

WRONG NUMBER

'Why can't we watch TV?' whined Leo. 'We always watch TV on a Saturday.'

'Because we have a guest,' said his father. 'It's not sociable. Why don't you play a board game with your sister and Makena? Scrabble or Monopoly?'

'Because they're boring games for old people. Why can't I play Minecraft or go on the Internet?'

'What has happened to your manners? I've told you ten times that the Internet is down. We're waiting

71

for the engineer. He can't come till next week.'

'You're in IT. Can't you fix it?'

'I don't work for the broadband company. I can't repair a cable under the street. Why can't you let this go? You're like a dog with a bone.'

'Because I saw you surfing the web earlier.'

'That was a video I'd already downloaded. Anyway, you shouldn't be so nosy. Go and fetch the Sudoku book. Then you'll be improving your brain. When I was your age, my mother used to tell me: "Flowers may bloom again, but you will never have a chance to be young again." Don't waste your time.'

Makena sat silently, pretending to read. Her stomach churned. Something was wrong. She too had seen Mr Ting on the Internet and knew for a fact the Wi-Fi wasn't down. He'd slammed shut his laptop as she went by but not before she'd seen the first few frames of a news report showing men in white biohazard suits and goggles. They were spraying the hut of a woman who lay comatose in blankets in Guinea on the coast of West Africa.

Makena's parents were hundreds of miles away, safe in Sierra Leone. If there was nothing to worry about, why were Shani and Mr Ting acting so weirdly?

Her parents had messaged twice. Once to say they'd arrived in Freetown and a second time to say that they were near Kenema with Aunt Mary, whose condition was worse than they'd feared. Five long days had passed since. Makena hadn't expected to hear much. Phone calls from rural Sierra Leone were expensive and the signal unreliable. But it didn't stop her from pining for them.

Li and Leo were squabbling about Sudoku. Makena read the same paragraph over and over, willing the hours to whizz by and bring her parents home on the five-forty a.m. flight on Sunday. When Shani's mobile pealed, her pulse quickened with hope. Shani picked it up and left the room before answering it.

She was gone a long time. A rash of nerves crawled beneath Makena's skin. The twins were sniping at each other and the toddler was demolishing a Lego castle with a toy sword. She'd hoped the call might be her mother.

A snatch of conversation reached her ear. 'Don't add that to your worries. Makena's happy and having a great time with Li.'

Makena sprinted down the passage and into the hallway, skidding to a halt in her socks and banging her knee on a table. 'Is that Mama, Aunt Shani? I have to speak to her. Please, I must speak to her.'

Shani held up her phone to show the call had ended. 'Sorry, Makena, your mother's phone ran out of credit. She's gone.'

Makena stared at her, aghast. Furious tears filled

her eyes. She wanted to scream at Shani for using up her mother's airtime when it was she, Makena, who so badly wanted to speak to her.

But before she could say anything, Shani was sitting her down and explaining gently that she had bad news. Aunt Mary had passed away. There were funeral arrangements to be made. Makena's parents would be in Sierra Leone for another week.

Makena was sad about her aunt and especially upset for her mother, but she had difficulty coping with the idea that it would be seven more days before she saw her mama and baba.

'So they'll be back on the twentieth?'

'Or the twenty-first. Depends when they can get a flight. Your mama wanted to speak to you herself but her phone started beeping and cut off. She said to tell you she loves you and misses you. Maybe we can try her in a couple of days. It would be better for you to speak to her another time anyway, when she is not so upset and doesn't have a headache. She has a lot on her mind.'

In the early hours of the twentieth, the nightmare she'd had on Mount Kenya returned. Makena was caught in the grey coils of an enormous snake. It was squeezing the life out of her.

She awoke in a snarl of bedclothes, gasping for air. Li, whose room she was sharing, was standing over her.

'Are you sick, Makena? You were moaning and you're very hot. Shall I get Mama?'

The last thing Makena wanted or needed was Shani making a fuss so she smiled, made an excuse and pretended to go back to sleep.

Soon the waiting would be over. Her parents

were due home in twenty-four hours. Life would go back to normal. Apart from when her father was climbing mountains and her mother was teaching science, Makena had no intention of letting either of them out of her sight ever again.

That day at school was pure torture. The hands on the cracked clock in her classroom crept forward with such lethargy that at one stage Makena was convinced time was moving backwards.

After netball that afternoon, she raced to the school gates to wait for Shani and Li. She was going to beg the Tings to take her to the airport that night so she would be there when her parents' flight got in at five-forty next morning. She'd sleep there if she had to.

As she paced up and down, she caught sight of the *Daily Nation* lying on the security guard's chair. The front page screamed: BREAKING NEWS: EBOLA OUT OF CONTROL. The photo showed villagers washing their hands under a red sign emblazoned: EBOLA KILLS!

The guard had his back to her. He was leaning into a car at the school gates and making notes on his clipboard. Makena snatched up the newspaper and hid behind his booth. She turned the pages in growing horror. One photograph showed a chalkboard planted in the yard of a grubby house. On it someone had scrawled:

POLICE ORDER
QUARANTINED
HOME
UNAUTHORISED
SHOULD
KEEP OFF

No one in the picture paid any heed to the notice. Chickens pecked in the red dirt. A toddler lolled beside a washing bowl full of suds on the porch. His mother hung washing on the line as if it were a day like any other. As if she hadn't been barred from entering her own home because a friend, neighbour or relative had died of a deadly disease in there.

Over the page, health workers in billowing white biohazard suits and elbow-length turquoise gloves carried a shrouded corpse on a stretcher. Dozens of crudely dug mass graves were lined up among the palms in what the reporter called the epicentre of the Ebola outbreak: Koindu, Eastern Sierra Leone.

Makena's breath torched her throat. If the virus was in Sierra Leone, that meant it had crossed the Guinea border and was moving like wildfire through the mangroves and red ironwood forests. Her parents and Aunt Mary were in its path.

Beneath the photo was a box of facts about Ebola.

EBOLA – A viral haemorrhagic fever causing
internal and external bleeding

TRANSMITTED BY:
Bats, apes and body fluids

SYMPTOMS:
Show two days to three weeks
after being infected

SIGNS TO LOOK OUT FOR:
Fever, sore throat, muscle pain, headaches

FATAL IN 50% OF CASES

She threw down the paper. Her mother had had a headache when she phoned. Makena staggered to the road. The security guard caught her as she fainted. She came to with Shani pressing a damp cloth to her forehead.

'It's all been too much for you, baby, first time without your mama and baba. I hope for all our sakes that they're home in the morning.'

Back at the house, Shani stationed Makena on the sofa, feet up and wrapped in a blanket. The Tings had planned a farewell barbecue in the garden for Makena but she was in no condition to eat or be cheerful.

'You must have a little something to keep your strength up,' said Shani, who didn't know about the newspaper report but did know that her young guest was in desperate need of some TLC. 'As soon as the veggie kebabs are ready, I'll bring you a couple. After we've eaten, we'll sit together and watch a DVD.

Choose something you'd like. Before you know it, it'll be morning and your mama and baba will be here.'

Makena waited until the whole family was out in the yard before throwing off the blanket and darting to the hall, where Shani usually left her mobile. She didn't care how much it cost or how much trouble she got into, she was calling her mother. She had to make sure that her parents were getting on the plane that evening.

The phone was answered on the fourth ring. To her surprise, music was blaring in the background. It sounded as if a party was going on.

'Mama?'

Male laughter boomed down the line. There was something on edge about it. 'MAMA? *Pikin*, dere are no mamas here. We in a *bar*. You have da wrong number.'

Makena dialled again. This time the phone rang only once.

'I tole you, *pikin*, wrong number.'

Makena found her voice. 'It's not the wrong number. I know it off by heart. How did you get this phone? Did you steal it? Where's my mother?'

'Who you calling a *tifman*?' the man said in Krio. 'You think I wan any business wit de *polis*? I pay *tree* weeks' money for… Hang on. Where you be calling from? Kenya? KWAME, NA EMAGENCY. TURN OFF DA MUSIC. Take yo *padi no do*.'

Bob Marley shut off abruptly. The laughter moved out of the room. When the man came back on the line his tone had changed. 'I beg pardon, *pikin*. Dis phone, I buy it on Kenema market. You saying it were yo mama's? So sorry to tell you, all dese phones, dey from dead people. Ebola, man, it be killing everyone. If dis market cat had yo mama's phone, she be gone, *pikin*. D.E.D.'

'Stop!' Makena was freezing and boiling all at once. 'I'm sorry for the people who died but they have nothing to do with my mama or me. I've made a mistake. I've called the wrong number. This is the WRONG NUMBER.'

Then Shani was prising the phone from her fingers and holding her tight and there was no longer anyone on the line. And Makena knew, with a crashing certainty, that now there never would be.

SHATTERED

'This is the house,' said Shani. 'It looks …
fine. I like what they've done with the
sunflowers. It'll be good for you to be
with family again, Makena.'

Makena didn't respond. Some days, most days,
it was too much effort to speak. Today was one of
them.

Samson Chivero had insisted on driving them.
He waited until a lorry had hurtled by, spewing black
smoke and dust, before parking outside a pink house
with a blue door. The paintwork looked as parched as

85

the fields they'd passed on the way to Isiolo in Kenya's drought-wracked north.

Despite that, an attempt had been made to create a mini front garden. There was a square of thirsty grass and a bed of scarlet geraniums. Two goats were trying to get at them through the wire fence. A tunnel of nodding sunflowers lined the concrete path.

They knocked twice before the door was flung open. A woman emerged in a clinging hot-pink dress. She had a baby on her hip and was strikingly attractive in a hard, coy way. Makena remembered overhearing Baba confide to her mama that, as a youngster, his half-brother Edwin had rarely been out of trouble. He'd only settled down when he'd moved to Isiolo and become a respected mechanic.

'Then he married the best-looking woman in the district and got himself a whole heap of other trouble.'

For a moment her aunt seemed to have forgotten they were coming. Then she seized Makena with her painted nails and crushed her to her breast. 'Poor, poor child. Priscilla's gonna take good care of you.'

Makena pulled away at the first opportunity. The baby smelled as if its nappy needed attention.

'You've missed Edwin. Some emergency at the garage. Probably a spark plug needed changing.' Priscilla waved a hand dismissively. 'Men!'

Inside there were more children: a boy of five and girl of seven. They all shared a room barely big enough to contain a narrow bunk bed and the baby's cot.

Shani's brow wrinkled. 'And Makena …?'

'It will be tough but we'll manage,' Priscilla sighed. 'In the beginning, she will have to sleep on the sofa or top to toe with my daughter. After that, God willing, some money will come in to help us finish the extension.'

She gestured towards the open back door. Through it they could see four breeze-block walls with wire and weeds poking out of the top. 'All it needs is plaster, paint and a roof and Makena can have a room of her own.'

'What about school?' Shani asked over tea. 'Makena has already missed so much. It's been over six weeks since her parents ... since ... You know, it's been hard. We tried to send her to her usual school but she couldn't cope. Too many memories. A change will be for the best, don't you think, Makena? New friends, new teachers.'

Makena had not spoken since leaving the car and she said nothing now. What difference would it make? Soon Shani and Samson would drive away, leaving her with these strangers. She'd met Uncle Edwin a handful of times over the years and remembered him as a tall, lanky and sweetly charming man. But she barely knew him.

From what she'd heard, he was not someone to

be counted on. 'Weak as water,' was the phrase her mother had often used.

Shani was still going on about school, as if it mattered any more. 'Makena is so bright and talented. She used to be top of her year at English and science. Her mother's hope was that she might one day go to university.'

'The difficulty is, now we have an extra mouth to feed,' said Priscilla. 'Things will be tight but, of course, we will do our very best for Makena. There is a first-class school in Isiolo. It goes up to eighteen years. Though there would be uniforms to buy, text books, exercise books, pens, shoes, hats, sports clothes, tennis rackets and trainers, swimming gear, netball . . . The list goes on. Some day if we are blessed with money we will send her there. Until then she will go to the local school. There are only two teachers for all ages, but what can you do?'

Uncle Samson cleared his throat. 'I can help. Not me, personally, but the New Equator Tour Company. We were broken-hearted by the loss of Makena's father, our finest mountain guide. We wanted to help his daughter. Our manager organised a charity auction and people were so generous in their donations. We thought of giving you a cheque but we didn't know your banking arrangements.'

He patted his jacket pocket. 'I have the cash. It should pay for a year at the good school and buy many of the other things you mentioned. Uniforms and such like. It might even stretch to the paint and roof for Makena's new room. Next year, we can try again to raise funds to put her through high school. It would be our pleasure to do this for Makena.'

He produced the fattest bundle of notes Makena had ever seen. Priscilla glowed. Uncle Samson's eyes widened as she spirited it into her bra.

'This will make all the difference. Once a person has money, the world is her oyster.'

They moved out to the vehicle. Uncle Samson had deposited Makena's rucksack and suitcase in the children's bedroom. They contained everything she owned in the world – clothes rescued by Shani from her old home, a few new ones, and shampoo, soap and toothpaste. Li had kindly given her three new books, bought with her own pocket money.

'I wish Makena could have stayed with us for ever,' said Shani. 'After six weeks, she's family to us. But we have four children of our own and my husband's business is struggling.'

'Do not concern yourself,' said Priscilla, all smiles now that her bra had won the lottery. 'Makena is in excellent hands.'

Like Uncle Samson, Shani had tears in her eyes when she hugged Makena goodbye. 'You know where we are if you need anything.'

The SUV was moving off when it suddenly screeched to a halt. Shani leaned out. 'Priscilla, I almost forgot to tell you, Makena is a vegetarian.'

'A veg what?'

'A vegetarian. She only eats vegetables, rice, beans, fruit and *ugali*. No meat, not even chicken or beef stock. She loves animals, you see. Sometimes she'll have a bit of fish.'

Priscilla's smile slipped. 'We will have to see what we can do. The problem is the cost of vegetables and fruit. The drought has pushed them sky high.'

Makena saw Shani bite back a comment. She opened her handbag and gave the woman all the cash she had. 'Will this be enough?'

'For now,' purred Priscilla.

Makena wanted to crawl into a hole in the barren earth. Since that wasn't an option, she forced a smile and waved goodbye to her friends. Seconds later, the dust had swallowed them up.

Priscilla took her by the hand. Her nails dug into Makena's palm. 'Come, darling, show us what you have in your suitcase. We can't have you keeping everything to yourself. In this family we like to share. There are no princesses here. You will have to help out too, same as everyone else. How are you with babies? My youngest needs his nappy changing.'

SLEEPING SPIDER

In the Tings' living room there'd been a magnificent silk tapestry of a heron eyeing koi fish in a lake. Reflected in the water were jagged-toothed mountains, wind-blasted trees and swirly bushes. One had to look really hard to see that amid the foliage lurked a tiger, poised to pounce on the luckless bird.

The tapestry was Mr Ting's pride and joy. He'd translated the Chinese characters for Makena: 'Coming events cast their shadows before them.'

Whenever Makena could get her tired brain to

function, which these days wasn't often, she wondered if she could have foreseen the tragic events in her own life. Had there been signs?

Maybe the nightmare on Mount Kenya had been a premonition after all. She should have listened to her gut and warned Mama and Baba that something terrible was about to happen.

If they'd refused to take her seriously, she could have faked a stomach bug and caused them to miss their flight or something. Even if they'd later rebooked, the extra day or two might have given them time to watch the news and discover that Ebola had reared its ugly head in some parts of Sierra Leone and become an epidemic. They'd have learned that many of the patients diagnosed with malaria were actually feverish with the Doomsday Germ.

Would they have gone anyway? *If you are brave for a noble cause, because you want to help others or fight for justice or save a life — perhaps even your own life — then being brave is the best thing of all,* Baba had told her.

Was entering a plague zone to save a life the right kind of bravery or the stupid kind? Makena didn't know. She did know that if her parents hadn't gone to Sierra Leone to try to save Aunt Mary, her aunt would have suffered and died alone. Makena could never wish that on anyone, least of all her aunt, who'd devoted her life to helping others.

Makena was not alone but she felt alone, which was the same thing. Most days she wished that she were dead too. That way, she'd be with her mama and baba and not in Isiolo, sitting on a cracked step under a dull sky, watching a fly crawl over her leg.

She waved at it half-heartedly but it returned five seconds later and she lacked the energy to drive it away again. She did, however, straighten the fly net over the baby's pram. When the baby fretted, she sang a spiritual that had been her favourite lullaby when she was younger. The lyrics were heartbreaking but her mother's beautiful voice had more than made up for it.

O my Lord, sometimes I feel like a motherless child
A long, long way from home

Makena was halfway through the song when she realised that now it was true of her. *She* was the motherless child a 'long, long way from home', just as the slaves who'd once sung it in America had been far from all they knew and loved in Africa. The words died in her throat but she didn't cry. For a few blessed moments she'd felt her mama's presence and heard her exquisite voice. She lived in fear of forgetting. She had the photo of her father, ice axe in hand, grinning as he dangled from a rock face, but of her mama she had nothing but memories.

The baby whimpered, bringing her back to the present. Makena squinted hopefully down the pot-holed street. Priscilla had promised to be back more than an hour ago.

Taking a tissue from her pocket, she blew her nose hard. The cold she'd caught from the younger children was getting worse. She'd been awake half the night because she couldn't stop coughing.

It was hard to believe that nearly four months had passed since the evening she'd phoned Sierra Leone. It felt like a lifetime. A life sentence. Time crept by at the pace of an ancient grandmother, marked only by the revolving shadows of the sunflowers or the demands of the baby to be fed and changed.

The 'first-class' school had never materialised. 'The money was not enough,' was all Priscilla was prepared to say on the subject. 'Pocket change,' she'd added with a sneer.

Makena noted that the pocket change seemed to have done very well in keeping Priscilla in stylish dresses and matching handbags and jewellery. She flounced out in them every other day when a dark, shiny car with a dark, shiny man at the wheel whisked her away for a long lunch. On her return, the clothes and necklaces went into a box under her double bed.

By the time Priscilla's children returned from school and her husband from work, she'd be in one of three outfits, the hot-pink dress or a simple one with orange and white checks. She also had a demure black and cream skirt and top with a matching cream hat that she wore on Sunday when the family attended the Kingdom of Fire Ministries.

Makena had been once. In Nairobi, her parents had been infrequent churchgoers. The chapel they'd attended when Baba wasn't travelling offered polite sermons about a kindly shepherd, and hot cross buns for tea.

The Kingdom of Fire was epic both in scale and emotion. Great cauldrons of *ugali* and stew smoked at the entrance. Scores of people came from far and wide to crowd into an old warehouse and blast the roof off with their praying and singing. At the height of the preaching, a gale-force love seemed to sweep the place. For the briefest of moments Makena had allowed herself to be caught up in it, then she reminded herself that if God had really cared for her he wouldn't have snatched away Mama, Baba and Aunt Mary. She'd refused to ever go again.

Priscilla, who in any case preferred her to stay at home with the baby, told Uncle Edwin that Makena was too traumatised to attend church or school.

'When she has recovered, God willing, she will catch up with her lessons. Until then, we must be patient. What does it matter if she has to repeat the year?'

And Edwin, who regarded his wife as a heaven-sent combination of a beauty queen and Mother Teresa, just smiled and said vaguely: 'Very wise, very wise. Yes, we can think about school when she's better.'

Makena wasn't holding her breath. Priscilla divided the world into two types of people: those who could be used and those who were a threat. Shani, Uncles Edwin and Samson fell into the first category. For reasons she could never understand, Makena fell into the second.

Part of the resentment was historic: Makena's mother had been a science teacher. Uneducated herself, Priscilla had a contempt for learning.

'Your beauty is your passport in this world,' she'd tell her daughter as she transformed her into a little doll each Sunday. 'Be alert for opportunity. *Aliye na hamu ya kupanda juu hukesha.* A person who wants to rise in society must stay awake.'

'Your *brains* are your passport in this world,' Makena tried telling the girl, but it was hopeless. She resembled Priscilla in more than just looks. A week after Makena moved in, the girl had given her a couple of hard kicks in the bed they shared, while pretending to be fast asleep.

Taking the hint, Makena had moved to the sofa. She'd been there ever since with the baby in his pram beside her. There were no spare blankets. At night she wrapped herself in a threadbare towel. She'd have done anything for the rock hot water bottle her father had made her on Mount Kenya. But comfort, like everything else about her former life, was a thing of the past.

That afternoon Priscilla returned in a taxi, two and a half hours late. Makena watched nervously from behind a curtain as she tottered unsteadily up the path, mouth pinched. Her mascara had run beneath one eye.

She barely glanced at Makena or the baby, just went into her room and reappeared in the faded orange dress. Her face was scrubbed bare of make-up and she looked oddly vulnerable.

She started banging around by the stove. Makena hurried to help. If she assisted with the cooking, she had a better chance of grabbing a bowl of ugali before Priscilla covered it in chicken or goat stew, which she often did out of spite. She knew it made Makena sick to her stomach.

As with the first-rate school, the promised vegetarian meals had never happened. Since Edwin ate lunch at the garage, the children at school and Priscilla goodness knows where, supper was a small, meaty meal or beans cooked with meat bones. Only occasionally, if her afternoon had gone particularly well, did Priscilla return with a pumpkin or *sukuma wiki* – collard greens – which she made with tomatoes, onions and many Kenyans' favourite flavouring: mchuzi mix.

That evening Makena was heartened to see Priscilla take the *sukuma wiki* out of the fridge. The vitamin C might help shift her cold. But when she went into the kitchen the greens were lying in a pool of blood. A lump of fatty meat of unknown origin was leaking into the leaves.

Makena's default setting these days was numb resignation, but her sinuses were killing her and she felt wretched and hungry.

Snatching up the bloody greens, she cried: 'Why do you do this? You know it means I can't eat them. Why do you hate me so much? I'm sick of this. I don't want to be your free babysitter and maid any more. I want vegetables and I want to go to school – the good school. The one Uncle Samson gave you cash for. If you don't send me, I'll phone him and tell him you've stolen the money. Then I'll tell my uncle—'

She never got any further. Priscilla gave her a swipe that sent her flying across the kitchen. She cut her cheek on the sharp handle of the low fridge. The other children were walking in from school. The boy burst into tears. The girl stopped open-mouthed.

'You ungrateful brat,' screamed Priscilla. 'After all we have done. We have taken you in when we didn't even know you. You were nothing to us. Now you have a roof over your head, food on the table and in time we were planning to send you to the best school. And you repay us with threats. *Usishindane na akushindao.* You should beware of challenging one who is more powerful than you.'

She stood over Makena. The knife she'd been using to trim the meat was still in her hand. Blood dripped from it.

'Did you think you could come here and lead a complimentary existence? You have seen how we struggle. Did you expect free lodgings, free water, free electricity? On top of that, you demand that we serve you your own special VEGE-FARIAN meals. As if you are royalty! And all the while you are like a viper in our midst. I have sympathy that your parents are gone but you are not unique. There are ten thousand orphans in Kenya. Sometimes I wish you had been lost in the car crash with your mother and father.'

For the first month after her parents had died, Makena had cried a river. She'd cried so hard and for so long that the river inside her dried up and left a hollow as arid and empty as the district in which she now lived. But at Priscilla's words a single, horrified tear fell from her eye.

She scrambled to her feet. 'What are you talking about? They didn't die in a crash. They died from Ebola.'

Priscilla sprang backwards, knocking the plates off the counter. They shattered spectacularly. Spears of china stabbed Makena's legs. Her aunt didn't even turn to assess the damage. Her hand was over her mouth.

'Ebola? *Ebola!* Edwin told me ... I didn't know ... oh my. Oh no ... and for the past three days you've been sneezing and coughing. You have brought this disease, this curse, into our home. You've been with my baby.'

Makena edged away. Her entire body shook with fear and shock. 'No. No, I just have a cold. I-I w-wasn't there.'

'Get out!' screeched Priscilla. She ran and lifted the baby from his pram, then gathered her other weeping children to her like a mother hen. 'GET AWAY FROM US AND NEVER COME BACK.'

As Makena stumbled out into the yard, the door was locked and bolted behind her.

THE WHITE LIE

When Edwin returned from work, he found Makena hugging her knees on the grass verge outside the house, shivering uncontrollably. Her cheek was swollen and there was dried blood on it.

'Who did this to you?'

'I fell.'

At first he could not get a syllable more out of her, but with patience he gathered the gist of the story. An uncharacteristic fury came over him. He lifted Makena and put her in his truck, covering her with his jacket.

'Stay here. Don't move, no matter what.'

The row that erupted was like nothing Makena had ever heard. She curled in a ball in the footwell of the truck, hands over her ears, but the battle cries of her relatives carried through the closed windows. Before crouching down, she'd seen people in nearby houses coming out on to the street.

'Don't blame Makena,' Edwin begged at one point. 'She is a child. I am the one who is in the wrong. I thought it was for the best. I worried that if I told you my brother and sister-in-law perished from this horrible disease you might not want her. It was a white lie.'

If he believed that admitting guilt might pacify his wife, he was wrong. She raged with increasing hysteria about how his lie had endangered her, his children and her precious baby. For days, Makena had been sneezing and coughing up lethal germs around the house. Even now, the virus might be working its evil in their veins. He may as well have dug their graves.

'You're talking crazy,' despaired Edwin. 'Makena never went to Sierra Leone. She was not with my brother or his wife. How can she have Ebola?'

'How do you know she never went? Were you with them? Do you have proof? The disease could have been lying hidden, like a sleeping spider, for months. How can I believe what you say ever again? How will I know if it is a white lie or a lie of another colour?'

Edwin pleaded and cajoled. He would take Makena to the hospital for tests and bring Priscilla a health certificate if that would satisfy her. Surely there was some way he could make it up to her, some way that they could work things out so that Makena could still live with them. She was alone in the world. She had nowhere else to go.

Priscilla was immoveable. 'She has her rich friends in Nairobi. It's her or me.'

After that the house was quiet for a considerable time. When the truck door eventually opened, Edwin was stooped and grey, as if the youthful marrow had been drained from his bones. He helped Makena on to the seat and put her rucksack at her feet. For several minutes he didn't seem to trust himself to speak.

'I'm sorry,' he said at last. 'Priscilla is a fantastic woman but she is a lioness when it comes to our children. She is scared for them. People in this area, many are ignorant. They have their superstitions around Ebola. They have filled her with fear. You know yourself, this disease can kill in a few days. Some people believe that those who cannot be killed by the virus are cursed or are witches. Priscilla is worried that if our neighbours discover we have an Ebola survivor in our home, they will cast us out on to the street. I could lose my job. It's nonsense because you were never with your parents in Sierra Leone but it is the way of this place.'

He said hesitantly: 'Your friends in Nairobi, are they good people? Do they treat you well?'

Makena nodded. It was obvious what was coming.

'Do you think they would . . . ?'

His hope hung in the air.

'Yes, I'm sure they would keep me,' answered Makena, because that's what he wanted to hear. 'If I could just get to Nairobi . . .'

The relief on his face almost made her cry again.

'No problem. One of our drivers – a decent, trustworthy man – is going to Nairobi early tomorrow to collect some parts. I will ask him to take you to your friends and make sure you're safe. It might be better for me to drop you at his house tonight. His wife will look after you and it will be easy for you to be ready at four a.m. Is there anything else I should fetch from inside for you? Do you have any other belongings?'

The rucksack was light against her leg. Makena thought of the stuffed suitcase she'd arrived with and shuddered at the memory of Priscilla and her daughter raking through her things. Some, she suspected, had been sold. She'd seen a girl at the store wearing the jeans and yellow Mount Kenya T-shirt Shani had bought for her. Makena's own jeans had gone missing and she knew the T-shirt was hers because the first and only time she'd worn it she'd managed to get a tiny ink stain in the centre of the O.

'There's nothing I want.'

Her uncle started the engine. 'Then let us proceed. In case you are hungry, I put some bread and two oranges in your bag.'

His sadness filled the cab like a mist. 'You are going too soon, Makena. With you here, I saw every day my brother. The best of him is in you. Keep strong, niece. Remember — however long the night, the dawn will break.'

♥

RUBBISH

'Stop! Over there on the left. By the jacaranda tree.'

For most of the four-hour journey to Nairobi, Makena had tried to doze. Her cheek still hurt but the swelling had gone down. The driver's wife had iced it, muttering darkly about Priscilla. She hadn't believed Makena's tale about tripping over a step. She'd also brewed her something foul-tasting for her cold. Whatever it was had practically cured Makena overnight, but it had left her feeling as if her head was detached from her body. She had the sensation of gazing down on herself from a great height and seeing a thin, broken child slumped against the lorry door.

Until a moment ago, her only plan had been to throw herself on the mercy of the Tings. She was sure they wouldn't turn her away. But as she roused herself from another miserable replay of the evening before, she realised that the driver was taking a shortcut down her old street. The home she'd last seen when she kissed Mama and Baba goodbye was zooming towards her. Makena's heart, a dead thing in her chest, pulsed for the first time in months. She came to life with a suddenness that startled the driver.

'Stop! Over there on the left. By the jacaranda tree.'

The driver was confused. He pulled off the road to check his notebook. 'This is not the address I was given by your uncle. We are nearly there. Another five or ten minutes, depending on traffic.'

'You think I don't know my own home?' said Makena, guessing, correctly, that her uncle would have avoided saying much about her background or her hurried departure.

'Sure, sure, you must know it. I also must be confident that you are safe. I promised Edwin. You are a young girl in a city of thieves and … Ah, ah! *Usitoke!* Don't move. Let me find a better place to park.'

But Makena had the door open and was jumping down into the street. As she rounded the front of the lorry, a man in a suit exited her home.

The lorry driver was in a panic. 'Wait, child! I will accompany you across the road. First, let us go together while I find a place to—'

'There's no need.' Makena waved to the man across the street as if he was a long-lost friend. He lifted a hand uncertainly.

She looked back at the driver, leaning from his cab. 'See. I'm expected. Thanks for the lift. You and your wife were so kind to me last night. Please thank her for the medicine. That's some powerful *muti.*'

The businessman met her at the gate. 'Do I know you?' he asked as the lorry growled into motion behind her. 'Are you a friend of my daughter's?'

Makena couldn't speak. She'd stepped on the spot where she'd last seen her parents and the past had sucked her into a vortex. Her father's voice echoed in her head. '*See you later, alligator.*'

She'd been laughing as she answered, '*In a while, crocodile.*' She'd been carefree. She hadn't known that 'later' might mean never again.

Her knees buckled beneath her. She sat hard on the muddy pavement. The man threw down his briefcase and wrenched open the gate, yelling to someone to bring some water.

'Are you ill? Shall I call a doctor or your family?' He took a phone from his suit pocket. 'Do you know your mama's number?'

Makena felt sick. She should never have come. 'I-I used to live here. My family used to live in this house. Now they're dead.'

The man looked uncomfortable. He tucked his phone away. 'We heard. I'm sorry for your loss. But what are you doing here?'

His wife came rushing up with a bottle of water. Groomed and perfumed, she had the harried look of someone with a high-pressure job. Her husband muttered something and she gasped.

'Can you deal with her?' he said under his breath. 'I'm late for a meeting.' He drove away without waiting for a reply.

The woman was nicer. She squatted in front of

Makena and took her hand. 'Would you like to come inside?'

Makena shook her head violently.

'Then what can I do to help you?' She looked up and down the street. 'Did someone bring you?'

Makena wiped her eyes with her sleeve. 'I left some things here. My mama's friend, Shani, she told me that the landlord sold everything – all our furniture, our pots and dishes, our pic…'

'Breathe. Take your time.'

'He got rid of our p-pictures and everything to c-cover the rent. Shani saved some of my clothes. What I want to know is, do you have the items that were on my bedside table? They weren't worth anything in money but they were special to me. They're all I have left of my parents.'

The woman became defensive. 'Look, when we came here, the place was a mess. The landlord is a criminal. He took our deposit and then when we arrived with our possessions nothing had been cleaned. I found a box of junk in the small bedroom. No toys. Just sticks and dirt and a jar of water. It was disgusting. I threw it all away.'

Makena let out a sob but no tears fell. She felt in that moment that she would never feel anything again. Nor would she have any reason to. Everything she had ever loved had been taken from her.

'That *wasn't* junk. It *wasn't* disgusting. Those were precious things my baba gave me – a leopard stick, volcanic ash and melted snow.'

The woman looked ready to weep herself. 'Sorry, sorry, sorry. I didn't realise. This breaks my heart.'

Then she brightened. 'Hang on, I remember now. I did keep one thing.'

Makena hadn't wanted to see how her home had changed but her feet carried her to the open front door.

When her parents had rented it, the house had been a cheerful space decorated with homemade cushions, batiks and worn but comfortable furniture. Teetering piles of pre-loved books bought by her mama with every spare shilling had doubled as coffee tables or homework desks. The radio was forever on. They'd danced to Pharrell Williams, clapping because they felt like happiness was the truth.

The house was silent now. No books were in evidence. Everything in the ordered lounge was sleek and pricey. Everything matched. The life Makena had shared with her family had been erased.

The woman returned with a framed photograph. It had been dropped, but Makena didn't care. Behind the splintered glass, that picture of her parents laughing on their wedding day was worth more to her than all the gold in Africa. She pressed its cool, sharp edges to her cut cheek and drew strength from her memories.

'Thank you,' was all she could manage.

There was a break in the woman's voice. 'You're welcome. I'm glad I kept it. It felt wrong to discard such a loving photograph.'

She glanced at her watch and swallowed a curse. 'I'm sorry but I must get to work. Who brought you here? Is somebody picking you up?'

Makena gestured airily at the street. She didn't want to lie but she didn't want to be watched over either. 'Any minute.'

'Maybe I should stay with you. There are plenty of troublemakers about.'

'*Hakuna Matata*. I've lived here most of my life. If anyone bothers me I'll get one of the neighbours I know.'

'You're positive? Then I'll go.'

She took some Kenyan shillings from her purse and pressed them into Makena's palm. 'Here, have this. Get yourself an ice cream or sweets – anything to make you smile.'

♥

Out on the street, Makena tossed the frame into a bin and added the wedding photo to the plastic sleeve that held the precious picture of her father climbing the Ice Window. Both went into the pocket of her climbing trousers.

She started walking. After the quiet of the north, Nairobi's rush hour was worse than ever. It was as if the city was staging a brass band parade made up of ten thousand tone-deaf players. By the time Makena reached the Tings' house, the elephant was not simply standing on her chest; it was trying to grind her into the dust.

Makena was dreading the moment when Shani answered the door to discover that her ex-colleague's daughter was her problem once again. She and Betty had enjoyed working together but had never been close. The only reason Makena had ended up with the Tings was because she and Li were friends and no one else could be found to look after her at such short notice.

Shani had already had to deal with far more than she'd bargained for. If she and Mr Ting did take Makena in, it would lead to the kind of rows about money and space (or lack of it) that had happened with increasing frequency in the weeks before she'd departed to live with her relatives.

There was also a risk that they would get the authorities involved. Well-meaning officials might take her into care or dispatch her back to Priscilla and Uncle Edwin.

As Makena tried to summon the courage to approach the house, Shani emerged with the children.

Li and Leo were neat and adorable in their school uniforms. Her friend skipped to the car with a book.

Makena ducked behind a tree. She waited until they'd driven away before moving on. They'd done all they could for her. Not for anything would she be a burden to them.

She began to walk aimlessly, in a daze of pain and loneliness. Borne along on the current of jostling, sweaty workers and hawkers, she felt shielded; part of something bigger. At Priscilla's house she'd been utterly alone, but in Nairobi there was safety in numbers. Cars, *matatu* taxis and bicycle owners could honk and rant as much as they liked but they couldn't run her down if she was crossing a road with twenty other people.

Everyone was going somewhere. She allowed herself to believe that she must be too. For a while she attached herself to a family, losing herself in a daydream where she still belonged. Eventually, the children started to stare and point. Trying to escape the pitying glare of their mother, Makena was almost crushed by a donkey cart.

She found herself in a street market. The air was blue with smoking pans of biryani and chapatti; beef knotty with gristle, blackened cobs of *makai*. She ducked under clothes-rails, squeezed between green hills of pumpkin leaves and bowls of dewy mangoes.

Emerging from beneath the plastic awnings and pink riot of Chinese toys, she noticed that thunderclouds were bearing down on Nairobi. Already they'd merged with a man-made cloud of oily black smoke rising from the distant slums. As far as Makena could tell, stuff was always burning in Kibera and Mathare. Warring gangs and slum dwellers experimenting with illegal electricity were the cause of many blazes. Fuelled by festering rubbish and crowded shanties assembled from planks, cardboard and rusting iron, fires could rage out of control for days.

The police and fire service seldom ventured into Mathare Valley and never at all into its worst neighbourhood, Nigeria Ndogo. They didn't dare.

Makena's feet had halted, of their own accord, at the steps of Blessings Hair & Beauty. She stared up at the salon on the first floor and had a sudden fantasy that all she had to do was climb the steps and sit in Gloria's chair and she'd be back on the Khumbu Icefall with Edmund Hillary and Tenzing Norgay. Her mother would interrupt her as she crossed an imaginary crevasse.

'What's up with you, Makena — do you have ants in your pants? How is Gloria expected to make a success of your braids with you wriggling and writhing in the chair?'

Makena would look up from her book and her mama would be leaning round the door, her expression a mixture of exasperation and tenderness. The nightmare of the past few months would be exactly that, a nightmare. She'd have dreamed the whole thing. Life would return to normal.

'Is that you, Mountain Girl?'

Makena started violently.

'Don't you remember me? I'm Nadira, Gloria's daughter. What happened to your braids?'

Makena's hand flew to her head. One sweltering, claustrophobic afternoon up north, when she'd once again been left alone with the baby, her grief had become so unbearable that the only way she could think of to deal with it was to rid herself of all reminders of the past, including the ones in the mirror. She'd cut off her braids with nail scissors.

When Priscilla returned from lunch with her secret friend, her reaction had not been what Makena was expecting. There'd been no scorn. No anger. Her gaze had moved from the rat's nest on Makena's head to the braids scattered on the floor. Empathy had skimmed across her face before taking flight.

Without a word, she'd scooped up the braids and put them in the bin, saying briskly: 'Let's get you tidied up.'

She'd combed out Makena's hair – roughly, but she'd done it – and trimmed it as best she could. 'Next time you want to try a fool thing like that, don't. When you damage yourself, when you destroy the body God gave you, it can't always be reversed.'

It was the last glimpse Makena ever got of the humanity and heartbreak that lay beneath Priscilla's brittle, beautiful shell.

Gloria's daughter came into focus. 'What's going on with you, Mountain Girl? Where's your mama? Do you want to come upst—'

Makena bolted, upsetting a table heaped with

dried beans. Shouts followed her as she dodged and weaved through the market. She wanted to run until she felt nothing and saw no one. Run until she reached Mount Kenya if she had to.

On and on she went, her too-small trainers slapping the crumbling streets. Dust and fumes struggled through her lungs. She slowed only when a stitch raked her side like a leopard's claw. Then she stumbled further.

When she was down to her last atom of energy, she bought an ice cream and slumped in a triangle of shade. She stared blankly into space, not thinking. The shadows deepened and moved around her.

Towards evening, the wind whipped up. Too late Makena tried to find shelter. There was little to be had that wasn't already taken. The storm, when it came, was a Nairobi-style deluge. Bomb-blast thunder. Strobe lightning. The streets gushed with muddy streams surfed by a flotilla of litter.

Somewhere far away was smart modern Nairobi with its gleaming malls and beautiful young professionals. Night would draw in swiftly and Makena knew she had to get back there if she was to have any hope of being safe.

Dripping and sniffing, she tried to get her bearings. A youth with glittering eyes stepped into her path and his friends jeered at her. Evading their clutches, she sprinted down an alley, rounded a corner and ran full pelt into a tree.

Then the tree shifted.

The hand that shot out and grabbed her wrist was the size of a goalkeeper's mitt and the forearm attached to it practically the width of her waist. Makena's eyes travelled up. And up. And up. Her brain struggled to comprehend what it was viewing through the rain.

She screamed and tried to leap away. The giant's head was among the storm clouds. Lightning illuminated it. Makena had a momentary image of a misshapen monster.

'Whatcha doing, psycho?'

The glittering youths were back.

The monster wheeled to lunge at them. Makena swerved away and was gone. She ran until she could run no more and then she limped. Her clothes streamed with water.

The storm was so fierce that it had driven all but the most desperate to shelter. Makena was barely able to hobble when at last she spotted a row of industrial skips behind a rundown brick warehouse. Beside them were two smaller bins, bigger than household ones but manageable. She tipped the rubbish out of one of them. It was mostly filled with paper but it hinted at a previous life when it had been a receptacle for fish guts.

Upending it, she crawled underneath. There was enough space for her to sit upright and use her rucksack for a cushion. It would keep her dry. A tear in the plastic side let in enough air for her to breathe but not enough to counteract the fishy fragrance. She tied her only spare T-shirt over her nose as a makeshift mask.

Her mouth was as dry as the fields around her uncle's house. She downed a bottle of water and the fruit her uncle had given her, pounding the oranges until they were soft, then drinking the juice from a hole she gouged in the top. She wasn't hungry. If she had been, the stench of the bin would have killed her appetite quickly enough.

Strangely, she was not afraid, not even after the incident with the Tree Man. She'd been more on edge living with Priscilla. She was quite proud that she had, on her own and in a storm, found shelter for the night to come. For the moment, that was her only concern. That, and putting on her dry sweatshirt before she caught pneumonia. It had a streak of blood on it from the cut on her cheek. That alone was a reminder that she was better off in a bin.

In the morning she would make a plan. There was bound to be one; she just couldn't think what it might look like right now. Her mind was a fog.

If the worst came to the worst, she'd go to the Tings after all. Or she'd turn up at the International School where her mother had recently begun teaching with Shani and appeal to their sense of charity. Perhaps they'd consider awarding her a scholarship. She could live in as a boarder and be educated for free.

The bin was parked against a wall. She leaned back and shut her eyes. Things would work out, somehow. Children from good homes didn't end up on the streets or in orphanages, did they? Those orphans were victims of war, famine or disease.

Like you, she couldn't help thinking.

Makena ignored the chorus of doubts in her head. There was a solution. She just had to figure it out.

The rain drummed a lullaby on the bin. Though she was cramped and cold, she slept.

Next thing she knew, she was being rudely awakened. The bin was plucked into space. Before she could move, someone had seized the hood of her sweatshirt and was bundling her up, ready to toss her into the maw of a garbage truck.

'Let go of me,' she yelled and had the satisfaction of nearly giving the bin man a cardiac arrest. 'Are you blind? I'm a girl, not a pile of unwanted clothes. Give me back my roof.'

'Your roof?' He stood scratching his head, framed by the crimson dawn. 'This bin is not your house. It's private property. Go back to Mathare. You should be careful where you choose to sleep. Next time we might throw you out with the rubbish.'

SNOW

In the last novel Makena and her mother had read together, orphaned boy wizard Harry Potter had used an Invisibility Cloak whenever he wished to disappear. In Nairobi, none was required. Twenty-four hours on the streets without access to a bathroom and clean clothes was all that it took for a girl to become a gutter rat and join the six hundred thousand-strong ranks of Mathare's unseen.

That's what the woman selling iced buns on the street corner called her — a rat. She eyed the bloodstain on Makena's sweatshirt and implied worse.

'I didn't *steal* the money,' Makena informed her crossly as the vendor took her damp, crumpled bills with distaste. 'My mama gave it to me. She's a science teacher, you know.'

And for a minute she could almost believe that her mother was still a science teacher and would be along as soon as she was done with her lessons.

The part about her mother giving her the money was true. It had been intended for Shani, to help with Makena's upkeep during her original six-and-a-half-day stay. Shani had refused it so Makena had hidden it in the pouch for valuables at the bottom of her backpack, ready to return to her mama when she came home. But Betty never did.

Scratching through Makena's belongings on that first, awful day in Isiola, Priscilla had somehow missed the money. Within the hour Makena had transferred it beneath a paving stone in the garden, for safekeeping. There it had stayed until Priscilla evicted her from the house.

The morning had not got off to the best start. Being mistaken for rubbish had a way of draining one's confidence. But it cheered Makena to think that the cash her mother had intended to help her was finally helping her, just when she needed it most.

Nearly two days had passed since her last proper meal, longer if she considered that her breakfasts and lunches at her uncle's house had consisted of bread and jam alone. She was ravenous. She did not intend to waste the money, but as she'd be on the streets for another day at most, after which she'd come up with a plan, she treated herself to a good breakfast.

She came away with two iced buns, two Cokes, a bottle of water, a banana and two vegetable sambusas. It was such a grand haul she could hardly carry it. All she had to do was find a place to enjoy everything away from prying eyes.

Her wild flight through the storm had got her thoroughly lost. In daylight it was apparent she was in what her parents would have termed a 'bad area'. It was far too close to Mathare Valley for comfort. Driving through Nairobi, her father had always taken detours to avoid the slum that sprawled over two kilometres. Makena had only seen it twice, through a shut window, her car door firmly locked.

Both times she'd been conflicted. Part of her was riveted with sad horror at the crush of rusting shanties that walled in the squalor as effectively as any fortress. The other half found it too hard to bear. That was the half that usually won. She'd avert her eyes as they swept by one of Africa's largest slums.

Now its tragic skyline was barely ten minutes' walk away. A ribbon of smoke twisted into the blue above it.

Makena hoped that her breakfast would give her the strength to jog the five kilometres back to downtown Nairobi. Or she could take a Matatu Madness taxi. Just as she was considering it, one did an illegal U-turn in front of her. It mounted the pavement, nearly mowing down Makena and a woman selling peanuts. The driver leaned on his horn, as if it was their fault for being there. He accelerated crazily away, his crammed-in passengers staring wide-eyed from the rear window.

Makena nixed the Matatu idea at once. She'd rather walk to Nairobi on blistered feet. More chance of arriving alive. Strange how her survival instinct had kicked in. At her uncle's house, she'd spent every other minute wishing she were dead. Now she wanted to delay that day for as long as possible.

The roads around Mathare overflowed with music, grime and life. The sambusas were cold by the time Makena found a picnic spot. A market stall not currently in use had been left on a quiet side street. An aged, ripped green tarpaulin was slung over it, weighted down with stones.

Makena hovered until she was briefly alone, then scooted under it. Beneath the cart it was clean and rather pleasant. She spread out a paper bag and laid out the iced buns, sambusas, banana and Cokes. She bit into an iced bun.

'Are you going to share that or hog it all to yourself?'

Makena almost choked.

An albino girl in a floppy hat leaned out of the shadows.

Makena recoiled. It's not that she didn't know about albinism. There'd been a girl in her class with the condition. Her parents were as black as Makena's but Mama had explained that albinism occurred when a rogue gene blocked the enzyme involved in the production of melanin – 'the body's paint palette'. The result was soft pink skin, a dusting of white-gold hair, and faded blue eyes.

Pigment aside, the girl at school had been no different to Makena or anyone else, but most of the children had ignored her. Some were mean to her because she didn't fit in and others shut her out because of superstitions that she wasn't quite human or that touching her would infect them with illness or turn them white. Makena had refused to sit beside the girl but not because she was an albino. To her, skin was just skin.

'Whether a person has stripes, spots or is as colourful and shiny on the outside as a butterfly, isn't important,' Mama had often said. 'It's what's underneath that counts. Are they courteous to others and kind to those who are weaker or less fortunate than themselves? Are they loyal to their friends? Do they stand up for what is right?'

Makena felt the same way. When she reeled away from the girl beneath the cart she was really recoiling from a shameful memory – the memory that she too had rejected the albino girl at school for the worst possible reason: because it was easier to follow the crowd.

She stuck out her hand. 'I'm Makena. Sure you can share my breakfast. If I eat all of this by myself I'll pop. I think my eyes were bigger than my stomach.'

The girl grinned and their palms met. 'Good recovery. I could write a book on all the thoughts that went through your eyes just then. That's okay. I'm used to it. I'm Diana, as in the Queen of the Supremes.'

'Who?'

'Diana Ross, Motown legend.'

In a strong, clear voice she sang a few lines from

songs about morning heartaches, Monday blues and getting by even when there were clouds in the sky.

'Heard of her but not the song,' said Makena, handing her new associate a sambusa, an iced bun and a can of Coke.

'Don't you know anything?'

'I know a lot. More than you, I bet. I like everyone from Rihanna and Freshlyground to Oliver Mtukudzi and One Direction.'

'*Who?*'

'Don't you know anything, Diana?'

She giggled. 'If we're going to be friends, you'd better call me Snow. That's my label around here.'

Makena was taken aback. 'You don't mind?'

'Why not? Snow is cool and not just in temperature. I saw it in a movie in the slum cinema once. These kids were rolling in it and building snowmen. It was beautiful.'

Makena found it surreal but also rather wonderful

to be discussing snow with a stranger under a market cart, one flap of a yellow-billed Black Kite's wing from Mathare.

'*I've* seen real snow on Mount Kenya. It was from a distance, but the early-morning sun was on it and it was a gorgeous, sparkling pink. Last time he climbed it, Baba brought me some actual snow from the summit of Batian. That's the highest of the three peaks. 'Course it had melted by the time it reached me but I didn't mind. That's what imagination is for. All I had to do was touch that jar and I'd be sitting on top of Batian in one second flat.'

It had been so many months since she'd allowed herself to think about the mountains she loved that even talking about them was a release.

Snow munched steadily through her feast, face enraptured. 'Where's your baba now?'

Pain filled Makena's chest like a vial of poison.

She had to force the words out. 'He . . . he and my mama passed away unexpectedly. One week they were here, next they were . . . gone. My Aunt Mary too.'

'What happened?'

Makena had a flashback of Priscilla reacting to the word 'Ebola' as if she were the Bubonic Plague in girl form. 'I don't want to say.'

'Sure, whatever. But just so you know, in Mathare, there's nothing new under the sun. How do you think the residents keep smiling? They arrive believing that whatever has happened to them is the worst thing in the whole world. Within hours they've learned the truth. Now they're thinking: "Compared to my new neighbour, I am truly fortunate."

'There's this girl I know whose parents were chopped to pieces in front of her in South Sudan.'

'Chopped to pieces?' Makena put down her bun, appetite gone.

'Uh-huh. Her story is tough to hear but there's always worse. You should see the child soldiers. They've escaped from *Al-Shabaab* or the Lord's Resistance Army or Boko Haram. Most are still babies but they shiver and shake and forget their own names like old men because they can't get the pictures of the terrible things they've seen and done out of their heads.'

She opened a can and took a long swallow. 'Famine, war, snakebite and malaria orphans, we've got them all. Then there are the Ebola orphans from Sierra Leone. We've been seeing more and more of those.'

'It was Ebola,' Makena burst out. 'That's what killed my mama and baba.'

Snow shrugged as if the Doomsday Germ was of no more consequence than the weather. 'That's life. Every now and then it springs a nasty surprise. That's why there are always at least three magic moments every day, to make up for it.'

'Are there?' Makena was doubtful. In the four months since she'd been orphaned, she couldn't recall a single one. The thought that there were thousands of children in more ghastly situations than hers brought her no comfort. Her own wounds were too raw. 'Why three magic moments? Why not two or twenty?'

Snow counted them off on her fingers. 'Sunrise and sunset, there's a couple right there. If I wake up scared and hungry in Mathare and life doesn't seem worth living if I'm stuck in the slum till I die, all I have to do is look up. The sun doesn't care whether it's shining on Mathare Valley or some gold skyscraper in the USA. It always brings its best costume to the party. Some sunrises take your breath away more than others but no two are the same. It's like the dawn is saying, "If I can be bothered to show up and treat each morning as if it's a fresh start, so can you."'

'How do you find the third magic moment?' asked Makena.

'It's already there, waiting. You just have to keep an eye out for it. Same with the fourth, fifth or twentieth. You're in one right now. Or I am, anyway.'

Makena was startled to find that she was too.

By lunchtime, Snow knew Makena's entire life story. Makena, on the other hand, knew little about Snow and was still too shy to ask. But in the middle of a competition to see who knew the most lyrics to the most songs, Snow suddenly said: 'You're wondering about me, aren't you? How I got here.'

'You can tell me when you're ready. I'm in no hurry.'

It was true. It was so long since Makena had had a friend to confide in that she was reluctant to leave the enchanted green space beneath the market cart to embark on the long, hot trek to Nairobi's centre.

However, when Snow started speaking, she could no longer contain her impatience. 'Begin at the beginning,' she said eagerly.

But Snow started in the middle, when she was twelve years old, with her midwife mother taking her to the place where she'd been born: Sumbawanga in the Lakes region of Tanzania.

It was election time, one year ago. In Tanzania, each new day brought a fresh report of Persons with Albinism being hunted down like antelope and killed or mutilated to order by witch doctors or their clients or apprentices. Politicians and other officials seeking power believed that albino body parts brought luck or riches.

They were not alone. Fishermen kidnapped albinos for their hair. They wove it into their nets, believing it would bring a bigger catch. Miners ground up albino bones and buried the dust, convinced it would turn into diamonds.

'Mama and *Bibi*, my grandmother, thought we'd be safest in our home village, away from the town where my mother worked in a clinic. We'd known these families all our lives. But on the first day the elders came to Mama and ordered her to dress me in black and leave me in a hut alone that night. They told her they wanted to perform a special blessing ceremony.

'Mama knew right away that they planned to abduct me and maybe kill me. There are places in my country and in Malawi where the Tribe of Ghosts – that's what they call us – are worth nothing alive. Dead, we can fetch as much as seventy-five thousand dollars. I'd sell a finger or a foot myself if I didn't think I'd miss it.'

Makena was aghast. She couldn't believe what she was hearing, much less that Snow was able to crack jokes about it.

'What ... what did your mama do?'

'She told them she needed to go to a nearby shop to get some black items for me to wear. Then she disguised me and put me on a bus with *Bibi*. I was clinging to her, begging her to let me stay. It was the last time I ever saw her. Next we heard she was dead. *Bibi* smuggled me into Kenya. We got as far as Mathare Valley before her heart gave out. The slum was too much for her.'

Inwardly, Makena was sickened beyond words. Outwardly, she showed little reaction. She had the feeling that that's how Snow coped, by making light of things.

Snow's eyes were bright with hurt and fury. 'She and Mama sacrificed their lives for me. One day I'm going to make them proud.'

Makena wanted to hug her but held back. 'You will make them proud. I know you will.'

Snow bit into an iced bun. She spoke through a mouthful, spraying crumbs: 'So where's the jar now?'

'What jar?'

'Your jar of snow.'

'Oh. The new people at my old house put it in the rubbish.'

'Then you have to make it your mission to get another. Everyone has to have a mission. Without that, why would they get up in the morning – except to see the sunrise? That can be yours. One day you'll fill a new jar with snow.'

'It wouldn't be same,' Makena said sadly. 'It wouldn't be the snow Baba gave me.'

'*Tch!* You wouldn't survive two days in Mathare if you went around feeling sorry for yourself. In the slum, we kids are the rubbish. You have to look forward to a day when things will be different or you go mad. The gift your father gave you, why does it mean so much to you?'

'Because he understood. He knew that there was nothing he could buy me from the mall – no music, clothes or even books – that would mean as much as snow he carried with his own hands from the summit of Batian. I'll never forget it.'

'If you'll never forget it, then it's not lost or broken. It's in your heart for ever. That means you're free to fill up another jar. Then you'll have double the joy.'

Makena stared at Snow. She'd never met anyone like her. Her words were bubbles of light, floating between them.

A police siren banished their magic moment. The street erupted into chaos. A scream, yells and the whip-crack of bullets. Running feet swerved by. Something struck their cart with such force the tarpaulin fell off, exposing them.

Makena ducked behind the rusty sign she'd been using as a backrest. 'What's happening?'

Laidback Snow had gone. She was on high alert, watchful as a wolf.

'Gang wars, that's what, between the Taliban — they're Luo, not the ones from Afghanistan, and the Mungiki, a Kikuyu sect. Some call them the Kenyan Mafia. They're going head-to-head over who controls the chang'aa business.'

'What's *chang'aa*?'

'Rocket fuel. That's God's honest truth. The gangs brew African moonshine out of molasses and millet or sorghum, then spice it up with jet fuel and battery acid. Sometimes they even use embalming fluid. You know, the stuff undertakers use to pickle bodies. It's vile but there are plenty in Mathare who can't get enough… Uh, we need to get out of here.'

She gripped Makena's hand. 'Now! This second, not yesterday.'

Makena tugged away. 'I've got to get back to the

city centre. I'm not afraid of the police. I've done nothing wrong.'

'You think they'll believe that?'

Two vans with flashing blue lights screamed past their cart. Tyres squealed. Riot police with shields and batons poured out. Muscular young men, buzzing like hornets, were massing at the end of the street.

Snow gripped Makena's hand and refused to let go. 'If we stay here, best-case scenario we'll be beaten, shot by mistake or taken away to the cells. Come with me to Mathare.'

'I'm not going to the slum,' cried Makena with real fear. 'No way.'

'You got any better ideas?'

'No.'

'Then run.'

LORDS OF MATHARE

Makena used her finger to rub her teeth hard with the paste she'd made out of wild mint and table salt. Snow had offered to share the snaggle-bristled toothbrush she'd found in a bin, but Makena drew the line at that.

She wasn't sure why. These days she routinely saw and did things that were so far beyond what she'd once considered acceptable they were on another planet. She even used 'flying toilets'. Three weeks ago, if someone had told her that night after night she'd do her business in a plastic bag and sling it into the Mathare River because it was too dangerous to brave the alleys after dark, she'd have said she'd rather jump off a cliff. Now it was the least of the slum's many challenges.

Still, using third-hand toothbrushes that had got up-close and personal with decaying chicken bones was not all right with her. It was good to have standards, she supposed.

Waiting in the queue to use the tap that smelled of sewage, Makena was almost glad her mother was dead. She'd never know the depths to which her daughter had sunk. That made no sense because if Mama were alive Makena wouldn't be in Mathare Valley. At this hour of the morning, she'd have been putting on her freshly washed and ironed uniform, ready for school. She'd have enjoyed a hot shower and cleaned her teeth with Colgate toothpaste and her own brush. But few things made sense any more.

On her first, mind-blowing evening in the slum, she'd had enough cash hidden in her shoes to keep her and Snow in collard greens, beans, rice, toothpaste and shampoo for a month, if they were careful and rationed treats. Snow had shown her how to keep the money safe from the spying, desperate eyes that saw everything in Mathare.

Actually, the money was gone in a day. With Snow trailing after her, pleading with her not to be such a *mjinga*-idiot-numbskull, Makena had blown the lot on all the buns, nuts and sweets she could afford. Fighting back tears, she walked the length of the slum handing it out to every hungry child she could find. Which was most of them. Next morning, she'd woken up hungry herself.

The slum kids nicknamed her 'Kissmass', their way of saying Christmas. Most afternoons they came to her for stories. A couple of girls had overheard her telling Snow about *Watership Down*. The tale of a rabbit family who are forced from their burrow and have to battle General Woundwort and his red-eyed rabbit troops and endure great trials in their search for a new home was one every Mathare child could relate to.

Next day, the girls who'd heard the story brought two friends and those friends brought others. Now no day passed without a story. Makena would perch on an upturned oil drum and tell thirty or more kids about *Charlotte's Web* or Hillary and Sherpa Tenzing's ascent of Everest.

She ached for the mountains the way she ached for her mama and baba.

The only mountains in Mathare were its rocky sides – the legacy of its past as a quarry – and the endless hills of rubbish. When it rained, the river overflowed and spread a toxic trail of plastic, broken glass and human waste. The smell was unspeakable.

Every now and then charity volunteers would descend and haul some of it away in bags, but it returned with the next storm, often within hours.

The sewage and chemicals leaked into the rusting, one-room shanty Makena shared with Snow and two other girls, Janeth and Eunice. Janeth's father had bought it before he died. It was two metres-squared and on the banks of the filthy river, the area reserved for the lowest of Mathare's low. When the river flooded, whole families were swept away.

The four friends slept in an untidy heap on a pile of cardboard. At night, rats as big as cats nibbled the edges and skittered over their limbs. Once a week, the girls washed their clothes in a single bucket of foaming river water. Makena's went in last. No matter how hard she scrubbed her sweatshirt and stained climbing trousers, they never lost their odour of sweat and despair.

On washing days, Makena sat around with Snow in her only spare T-shirt and underwear, waiting for her wet things to dry. She and Snow were lucky to have anything spare. Janeth had to hide in the shanty in the nude until her clothes were partially dry. On rainy days, she didn't leave the shanty at all.

Few shanties were more than a hand-width apart. Makena could not only hear the woman in the shack on the left crooning to her baby or scolding her boisterous sons, and the man on the right snoring like a chainsaw, she knew the gossip of families who lived five doors down.

She was aware, for instance, that the gaunt teenager who lived with his mother three shanties along was rather too fond of the local moonshine. Most mornings he could be found slumped outside his mama's shanty, mouth open for the flies to inspect. After seven straight days of watching him sleep away the mornings and doze all afternoon, Makena joked: 'I guess the last batch of *chang'aa* didn't contain rocket fuel.'

It was the only time she ever saw Snow angry. 'You think it's funny? All it takes is one bad brew and he'll die. That's what *chang'aa* means in Swahili: "Kill me quick."'

Within the week, the bad brew had happened. The youth was taken away in a box, his mama wailing behind it. The shock of his passing killed her days later. Death was so commonplace in Mathare that the neighbours barely turned their heads. An hour later, a new family had moved into their shanty.

It enraged Makena that the gang members were allowed to get away with openly cooking up the spirit in jerricans on the banks of the river. They mixed the filthy water with *chang'aa*'s already lethal ingredients. The illegal brew was worth millions to the gangsters and the corrupt officials who let them get away with it. They swaggered around the slum in diamonds and gold jewellery: Lords of Mathare. Each was wealthy beyond his greediest ambitions. None cared that they were tormenting some of the poorest people on earth.

Day after day, Makena rose fully intending to come up with a concrete plan to return to 'normal' life. She was convinced there was a solution. A family friend would take her in. Either that or she'd hitch a ride to Mount Kenya and live in the foothills gathering honey and firewood to sell, just as her father had in his youth. She'd save up until she could afford to go to school again.

But the process of getting ready to face the world every morning was an exhausting one in Mathare.

There was the daily struggle to find food with little or no money when half a million others were trying to do the same. Makena became an expert at spotting the lone onion or squashed tomato that had escaped under the table of one of the vendors on the roads beyond Mathare. Snow knew which shop bins had not already been raided for cartons of sour milk or blackened plantains.

Whether they returned with two shrivelled carrots or a handful of monkey nut shells, Eunice would conjure up a watery soup with the help of a few dried beans and *mchuzi* mix spice. Janeth had occasional work as a maid and on those days she picked up *nyama choma* (roast goat) for herself and Eunice. Like Makena, Snow never touched meat, so Eunice brought them *ugali* or *sukuma wiki*. It was a rare indulgence.

Some days they didn't eat at all.

They survived, after a fashion, but there was little energy for anything else. Eunice's cracked mirror showed Makena that her hair was growing out in tufts. Her collarbones jutted. Her T-shirt hung loosely against her ribs.

Whenever she tried to picture herself turning up at the International School to beg for a scholarship, her imagination took a holiday. Why would anyone take a chance on her? She kept putting off until tomorrow the long walk into town. She worried that tomorrow might never come.

Finally, it was Makena's turn to use the tap. She splashed her face and rinsed the mint and salt from her mouth, grimacing at the foul water.

As she bent to scrub herself with a sliver of cracked soap, using the puddle at her feet as a mirror, a memory came to her. The sting in her cheeks as she washed her face in clear, sweet Lake Rutundu on Mount Kenya. The blur of water in her eyes and then, like a miracle, the bat-eared fox. It was so vivid; so real. She saw it lift its head and turn a fearless gaze on her. There were water diamonds in its whiskers.

An inhuman growl blasted the image away. She swung round, heart thumping. Children were scattering like quelea birds before a farmer's shotgun. One boy stayed long enough to tug at Makena's shirt. 'Kissmass, run. the Reaper is coming.'

It was too late. The sun was blotted out. The Tree Man loomed over her. 'You!' He crushed Makena's arm with a hot paw. 'I remember you.'

Makena screamed. Snow, who was in mid-yawn as she stepped out of their shanty, snatched up a broom and raced to her friend's rescue.

Out of the corner of her eye, Makena saw something spark and shimmer. The giant saw it too. His grip loosened.

The soap on Makena's arms helped her twist away. She took off, grabbing Snow's hand as she ran. The albino girl knew the byways of the slum like she knew the lifelines on her own palm. They were out of sight in seconds. For ages afterwards, they could hear the giant stamping up and down in a rage.

'That's the Tree Man I was telling you about,' Makena whispered to Snow. 'The one who grabbed me in the storm.'

Snow stared. 'And you got away? That's twice now. Better not let the Reaper catch you a third time.'

A chill went through Makena. 'Why do you call him the Reaper?'

'Because wherever he goes, children disappear. He's soft in the brain and only following orders, but they say he works for someone high up who knows exactly what he is doing. A man who drives a Mercedes with blacked-out windows and no number plate. In Mathare, they call him the Diplomat. If the Reaper is on the look-out for you, you need to watch your back. Stay close to me. As long as we're together, you'll be safe.'

Makena experienced a jolt of *déjà vu*. Hadn't Baba said the same thing when the hyenas were circling? He'd been so busy keeping watch over her that he'd forgotten he needed saving himself. Now he was gone. Would the same thing happen to Snow?

Makena refused to allow that. If Snow was going to take care of Makena, Makena was going to guard her too. This time when the hyenas came hunting, she'd be ready.

POPPIES

It was Snow who remembered Makena's birthday. There was a promotional calendar on the wall of their shanty, illustrated with photos of Kenyan wildlife. June's animal was a warthog. When Snow blasted her awake on the third, belting out Stevie Wonder's birthday anthem as if turning twelve in Mathare Valley was an event worth celebrating, Makena's gaze went straight to the warthog. It looked the way she felt. If she'd had a pillow, she would have buried her head under it.

But Snow was irrepressible. Even their roommates,

171

rubbing sleep from their eyes, were smiling. They sang in Swahili:

Afya njema na furaha
Afya njema na furaha
Afya njema na furaha mpendwa wetu, Makena
Afya njema na furaha mpendwa wetu, Makena

Maisha bora marefu
Maisha bora marefu
Maisha bora na marefu mpendwa wetu, Makena
Maisha bora na marefu mpendwa wetu, Makena

'Today is going to be a day of at least six magic moments, starting with the dawn,' declared Snow after they'd wished Makena good health and happiness and a long and fruitful life. 'I've just peeped out and the sun has put on his best scarlet finery especially for you.

After you've watched his show, we've clubbed together to pay for a shower for you in the public bathroom. First, though, you have to open your gift.'

She handed Makena a parcel wrapped in newspaper and tied with string.

Makena was deeply moved. Snow had nothing. In fact, she had less than nothing. Makena knew how much thought and effort would have gone into finding clean newspaper and string, let alone whatever was inside.

'Open it!' urged Janeth. 'I can't bear the suspense.'

Makena removed the paper as if it was gold leaf not the sports page of the *Daily Nation*. Inside was an empty jam jar. A label made from a torn scrap of cardboard had been tied to the lid: 'FILL ME WITH SNOW'.

Her roommates were shaking their heads. 'An empty jar? We are poor but you would have been better off giving her nothing. What snow is she going to fill it with, Diana? Are you going to climb inside?'

Makena was so choked up she could barely speak. 'It's a long story and one for another day. But I promise you that if Snow was a millionaire, she could not have bought me anything more special than this jar.'

She hugged her friend tight. 'Thanks, Snow. I'll keep it always. One day I'll find a way to fill it.'

In Mathare, there were two types of people. Those who lived by the motto: *Mwenye meno makali ndiye mmaliza nyama*: the person with the sharpest teeth is the one who finishes the meat. And those who believed the saying *Msafiri mbali, hupita jabali*: one who travels widely will pass the mountain.

To Makena's amazement, most people fell into

the second category. The rays of light and love that shone through the darkness of Mathare were a source of daily wonder to her. Hope was everywhere. It found its way up through the dirt and desperation like a wildflower struggling through a crack in an inner-city pavement.

The slum school nearest her shanty bore no resemblance to the one she'd attended. Optimistically named Success Academy, it was more barn than place of learning. Sheets of rusting iron were welded together to form a long, narrow structure barely bigger than Makena's old classroom. Two hundred children crowded into it. There were no desks or chairs. Girls and boys of all ages sat on the dirt and shared a single toilet – a putrid hole in the ground with a metal screen.

Despite this, the pupils smiled more readily than any she'd ever known and the teachers were smartly turned out and dedicated.

One newly qualified teacher lived near Makena by the river. Every day she emerged beaming from her rickety shack and set off to the school. Makena watched her go with a lump the size of a golf ball in her throat. Some mornings it was all she could do to keep from running up to the woman and sobbing: 'My mama was a teacher too.'

Many slum women scraped a living selling bags of grain or beans, or making crafts from scavenged soda cans, cloth and leather. They nodded over their wares late into Mathare Valley's firelit evenings, hoping a customer less poverty-stricken than themselves would help them feed their hungry children.

It was deadly business. Nightly, they ran the gauntlet of the dreadlocked, machete-wielding *Mungiki*. The Taliban, who prowled the alleys seeking 'protection money' from slum residents, could be just as brutal. The lives of these women were short and unimaginably hard, yet they laughed more often and with a more intense joy than any Makena had seen out shopping in the fancy stores of Nairobi.

As she and Snow picked their way through the crowded, broken alleys that afternoon, the red dirt squares between rang with cheers and groans as the boys fought fierce games using a *jwala*, a football made from tightly wound plastic bags and twine.

Every boy in the slum dreamed of wearing the green and yellow uniform of Mathare United Football Club, one of Kenya's top teams. The best showed off their skills in the hope they'd be spotted by scouts from Manchester United and other legendary clubs. For most, it was their only chance of ever escaping the slum.

Snow gave a live commentary on the game as they walked. Makena barely heard her. She'd been in the slum nearly a month but she'd never lost the feeling of being prey, and not just because she was scared the Reaper would come hunting for her. There were eyes watching in every corner of Mathare Valley. Many were friendly or indifferent, but some were calculating.

Makena feared more for Snow than for herself. Mathare Valley was packed with refugees from countries such as Tanzania and Malawi where children with albinism were being kidnapped daily. She'd heard whispers in the slum, where some talked of Snow as a 'zero' or an 'invisible'. Snow pretended not to hear them, but the night sweats she suffered betrayed her secret terror that she was worth more dead than alive.

They passed the last of the shanties and climbed the rocky path to the rim of the crater in which the slum sprawled. When they reached the grassy summit, the view left them spellbound for all the wrong reasons.

Seen from above, the shanties and mud shacks were packed so closely together that they appeared to share a single roof. A pall of smog and *nyama choma* cooking smoke hung over it.

'Mathare's other name is Kosovo,' Snow told her. 'You know, like the European country where they had a big war. When people in Mathare saw the bombed-out buildings and concentration camps on the news, they said: "That looks just like our home!"'

Surrounding Mathare were tilting blocks of social housing, crumbling and riddled with crime. Between them were still more of Nairobi's two hundred slums, more pits of lawlessness and misery. Kibera, Nubian for 'forest' or 'jungle', was the largest in Africa and among the biggest in the world.

Makena shivered, not just at the sight of them but because she had cramps. Janeth and Eunice had given her a bag of hot *mandazi* – pillowy, deep-fried pyramids of dough dusted in icing sugar, all to herself. Her stomach was in shock. It hadn't been full for weeks. A film of sweat shone on her skin.

The cramps faded and she smiled at Snow. 'Thanks to you, Eunice and Janeth, I've had five magic moments already today: a snow jar, a beautiful sunrise, a shower, *mandazi* and *The Karate Kid*.'

They'd had a fun afternoon at the Slum Cinema, watching Ralph Macchio defeat his Cobra Kai opponent on a crackling, pirated DVD.

Beneath her floppy hat, Snow was rubbing aloe on her arms and face to soothe the sunburn on her pale skin. 'You have at least one more magic moment to come. There's the sunset, obviously, but I think we can stretch to a couple more.'

She fixed Makena with one of her intense looks. 'You miss your mountains, don't you?'

'A little,' admitted Makena. To her, the mountains

and her father had been one and the same thing, as if the same ancient lava crackled through their seams.

'A lot. What did you say the highest peak on Mount Kenya is called? Bat something.'

'Batian.'

'Right.' Snow sprang lightly up to the summit of the tallest heap of rubbish. 'Come up here. Let's pretend we're sitting on top of Batian.'

Makena joined her reluctantly. 'That takes a huge leap of imagination.'

'That's why I gave you my gift – to help you make it. Didn't you say that all you had to do was touch your jar of melted snow and, in your mind, you'd be sitting on top of Mount Kenya?'

'I did.'

'Well, then?'

Makena couldn't help laughing. She took the jam jar from her backpack, held it between her palms and closed her eyes. Blanking out Mathare Valley and the smell of rotting rubbish, she pictured herself sitting beside Lake Rutundu, breathing in the herby smell of heather. Snow glistened on Mount Kenya's peaks. All around her was mauve-tinted moorland and eagles wheeled overhead.

A rowdy group of boys brought her crashing down to earth. They began searching through the heaps nearby.

Makena gave up on her vision but not on her ambition to some day fill her jar with snow. She nudged her friend. 'You're always telling everyone else to have a mission. What's yours?'

A dreamy expression came over Snow's face. 'I want to dance on a stage and have my name in lights like Michaela DePrince.'

She dug in her skirt pocket and pulled out a page from a magazine. It had been folded so often it was ready to disintegrate, but Makena had no trouble making out a black ballerina in a brilliant pink tutu. She appeared to be flying – actually flying – over the red brick buildings in New York City.

'That's Michaela,' Snow said proudly. 'Isn't she beautiful? She was a war orphan from Sierra Leone.'

'A *war orphan?*'

'Uh-huh. When she was four, this magazine picture of a ballerina dancing *The Nutcracker* blew into her orphanage. She made up her mind that one day she would dance and be happy like the girl in the picture. Her teacher was killed in front of her and so many bad things happened to her, but finally some kind Americans adopted her. Now she's a dancer with the Dutch National Ballet and I'm looking at her photo and dreaming of being happy like her. After I read her story, Mama bought me a ballet book and I taught myself some moves. It's a circle.'

Makena admired the picture. The young woman was so graceful and strong. 'Have there been any albino dancers?'

'Hundreds! There've been albino singers and actors and athletes too. Some are famous but those aren't always the best. No one ever thinks about the nameless ones because they don't sell expensive tickets, but a lot of them have done things that are far more important. They've helped people who are hurt or made war children smile. These are the legends in the real world – *our* world.'

'But you still want to be on the stage with your name up in lights?'

'Yes,' Snow cried passionately. 'Not because I want to be rich and famous, although that would be cool, of course! More because I want to inspire people the way Michaela has done.'

Makena decided right then that when she grew up

she too wanted to inspire kids to be proud of who they were. She wasn't sure how, but she'd think of a way.

Snow nudged her. 'Read Michaela's story out loud. Reading's hard for me. The words go back-to-front and sideways. They dance, but not in a good way.'

'You can get help for that,' Makena told her. 'Glasses or contact lenses.'

'Here? In the slum?'

'Maybe not here but when you're a dancer on stage.'

'Okay, I will. Now tell me what the story says.'

Halfway down the page Makena came to a quote from Michaela. 'The corps is the backdrop to the story—'

Snow giggled. 'It's not corpse as in dead person. It's "corr", as in *corps de ballet*. It's French. In the book my mama gave me, it said that's the name for the ballet dancers who dance together as a group. The soloists,

185

the principal dancers, are the ones who get all the attention, but the *corps* is like a family. They belong to each other.'

The page blurred before Makena's eyes. She'd once belonged.

She struggled on: 'Michaela says: "The *corps* is the backdrop to the story, a forest, a snowstorm, a flock of birds or a field of flowers. One red poppy in a field of yellow daffodils draws the audience's eyes to the one poppy. However, I don't think the answer is to cull the poppy. I think it's to scatter more poppies about the field of daffodils."'

Snow tucked the article into her pocket. 'That's what I'm going to do. I'll be a red poppy scattering the seeds of hundreds more poppies.'

THE REAPER

'Can I have one last request?' asked Makena. 'For my sixth magic moment, I mean. Would you dance for me? The sunset can be the backdrop and maybe me and those little kids coming up the hill can be your *corps de ballet*.'

Snow lit up like a boxful of stars. 'Really?'

'Yes, really.'

Snow called to the eldest boy on the next-door rubbish heap. 'Hey, Innocent? What tunes do you and your crew play?'

He strutted across, drumming a rhythm on a tin can. 'We know everything.'

'We're doing Slum Lake. *Swan Lake*, only in Mathare. It's a ballet by Tchaikovsky. You wanna play for us?'

'Sure thing. We don't know no Chomsky but if you're talking 2face Idibia, Pharrell, Akon, Beyoncé, Ladyship Black Mambazo, we've got the beats.'

Makena wasn't a dancer. 'Two right feet,' her mama used to tease. 'Right for climbing but maybe not for dancing.'

Snow wouldn't take no for an answer and before Makena knew it she was following her friend's flying feet (sort of) as she performed *allegro* and *cabriole* leaps. Innocent's band sang and drummed up a storm on buckets, tins and a homemade guitar, and the sun set in a wildfire blaze over the rubbish heaps of Mathare Valley.

Children came running from every part of the slum. Their audience grew by the minute. But it was Snow who was the star of the show. She never tired. When night descended and Mathare's cooking fires and illegal lights flickered uncertainly to life, Snow became a girl of myth; free of gravity.

Thunder blasted, bombshell loud. Makena, who had sat down because her stomach hurt, felt the ground shake beneath her. Lightning snaked across the dump. It illuminated Snow as she flew through the air, suspended above Mathare Valley just as Michaela had been over Harlem.

A bulldozer ramped over the hill, dazzling Makena with its lights. A tsunami of rubbish came with it. Dirt spat in her eyes. Trying frantically to evade the crushing treads and stampede of children, she went tumbling down a dark slope. Unable to halt her fall, she rolled until she hit the road below, twisting her ankle.

The pain was electrifying. For a minute, she thought her ankle was broken. It ballooned in an instant, making hobbling difficult and running impossible.

A second bulldozer arrived and began demolishing a line of shanties. Its progress was overseen by aggressive, shouting men. Panicked residents were running everywhere. Police sirens added to the din. A security guard spotted Makena and moved threateningly towards her.

Makena gritted her teeth and half-jogged, half-limped out of range. A chaos of children came flying from the slum. 'Run, Kissmass!' yelled a girl from her story group. 'Run with us.'

'Where's Snow?' called Makena. 'Have you seen Snow?'

A police car screamed into the street, drowning her words. The children sped off. Makena followed as fast as she could. People were tearing in every direction, some dragging possessions, but she couldn't keep up with any of them.

She became increasingly panicky and disoriented. A family tried to take her with them but gave up when Makena had to stop to rest her ankle. When she rounded the next corner, she was alone.

Her stomach cramps had returned and a headache hammered at her skull. She hoped she didn't have cholera. There'd been an outbreak in Mathare. Health workers had been distributing leaflets warning people to wash their hands regularly with soap and avoid buying street food. The *mandazi* now seemed a mixed blessing.

Given the state of her foot and stomach, Makena decided that her best and perhaps only chance of surviving the night would be to do what she'd done that first night alone in Nairobi: find a bin and sleep beneath it.

In the morning, she'd return to Mathare Valley and find Snow. She'd convince her friend to leave the slum. They could hitch a ride to Mount Kenya and live off honey and foraged roots and leaves. Snow was talented and resourceful and Makena understood mountains. Together, they'd thrive. And when they were old enough, they could save up and go to the UK or Europe, where Snow would become a famous ballerina.

Anxiety added to the cauldron in Makena's stomach. She kept seeing Snow suspended in mid-air as the bulldozer crested the rise. Had her friend escaped its crushing treads and great metal jaw, or had she…?

No, Makena refused to allow the thought to take up residence in her brain. Snow would be as angry and sad as everyone else in Mathare Valley. She'd no doubt have a few cuts and bruises. But she'd bounce back. That was the thing about free spirits: they were indestructible.

It was then that Makena noticed the Mercedes. It was idling by the side of the road, dust motes twirling in the red glow of its rear lights. There was no number plate on its bumper.

Terror paralysed her. If the Diplomat was here, the Reaper wouldn't be far behind. They were probably on the look-out for lone children.

Lost girls like her.

Like a beast from a fairy tale, an immense silhouette unfurled from behind the car. The Reaper had been leaning down, out of sight, talking to the driver.

Makena dropped to the ground, desperate for somewhere to hide. Almost immediately, she recognised the street opposite. It was the one where she and Snow had picnicked on the day they met. If she could get to it without being seen, she might be able to hide under the market cart. She prayed it was still there. Either way it was a risk. The street was a dead end. If the Reaper or the Diplomat spotted her, she might end up trapped.

The monster leaned down again, summoned by the driver. Makena crawled behind a low wall and inched forward. She was in luck. The cart was standing in the shadows, a tarpaulin hanging over it.

The Reaper straightened. He strode away in the opposite direction.

It was now or never. Makena made a break for it as speedily as her swollen ankle would allow. Unfortunately, the cart was further along the street than she remembered. Each step and every breath was pure torture.

She was almost there when she tripped over a can concealed in the darkness. Its tinny clang reverberated along the silent street like a cymbal smashed by a drummer.

Makena dived under the cart. Nothing happened for a moment. Then she caught the muffled thud of running feet. Her head was spinning; her heart slammed her ribcage. Had the giant seen her or not?

He was walking now, his footsteps stealthy and sure. She could almost hear him smile. There was nothing she could do. Nowhere she could limp or crawl. She'd run out of options.

The Reaper stopped beside the cart. He lifted the tarpaulin and reached in.

SHIMMER

Twenty minutes earlier, on the Meru–
Nairobi Highway, Helen Stuart had clicked
off her phone and run a hand through her
messy auburn bob. 'That's it,' she told her
companion in the backseat of the Hearts4Africa
Land Rover. 'Official confirmation from Matron.
We're overflowing, over-capacity and, as per usual,
over-budget. Every bed, sofa and spare mattress is
occupied. We should go home. Don't know about you
but I'm so exhausted that I'm ready to check into The
Best View.'

The quirky names of Nairobi's street hotels and restaurants were a standing joke between her and Edna Wahome. The Best View, in particular, made them laugh. It was a rainbow-hued shack facing a concrete wall.

Neither of them knew how the teetering assembly of red and green metal and candy-striped awning that was The New Boiling Soup Hotel had come by its title but they enjoyed trying to guess.

'Perhaps The Old Boiling Soup Hotel went out of business because their sweet and sour soup was lukewarm,' suggested Edna.

Her own favourites were the ones with creative spelling: The Exelent Motel and The Foward Thinking Inn. Helen liked the optimistic ones. The Hotel Majestic was a chicken coop painted sky-blue and Mama Africa's Finest Suites were three breeze-block rooms, crudely decorated with flowers and lions. Both women loved The Funky Monkey Inn.

As they crisscrossed Kenya, they had an ongoing competition to see who could find the hotel with the funniest name. It was a silly pastime but it made them smile. In their line of work they needed all the smiles they could get – this week more than ever.

At two a.m. on Monday, bulldozers had descended on Kibera slum. A property developer had purchased a corner of land and wanted it cleared. The landlord he bought it from had taken the money and run without mentioning it to his tenants. In the dead of night residents were chased from their shanties with no warning or notice. To see them picking through the rubble in daylight – weeping for the loss of their meagre possessions, homeless with nowhere to go – was devastating. Edna and Helen had spent three days trying to put a feeding programme in place for the children.

Tonight, a Thursday, it had been the turn of Mathare Valley. Bulldozers had crushed more than fifty shanties. As always, it was the orphans who suffered most. It was those orphans – particularly the girls – that Edna and Helen wanted to help.

For the past fifteen years, they'd dedicated their lives to Kenya's forgotten children. They'd met while volunteering for an international charity. Newly arrived from the UK, Helen was fresh out of university and already besotted with Africa. Edna, a Kenyan, had recently qualified as a nurse.

They'd hit it off on day one. It helped that they had the same dry sense of humour and stubborn belief in justice.

They'd quickly become disillusioned with the charity. Hard-won donations were frittered away on shiny new vehicles when second-hand models would have done just as well. Corporate sponsors were treated to luxury safaris. Charity bosses received bonuses that could have kept whole villages in food and medicine for years.

After a row with her manager over a lunch paid for with donations meant for orphans, Helen had walked out. Edna had walked with her. Over a consolation *chai* tea, they'd hatched a brave and crazy plan. They'd start their own Kenyan orphanage and give hope to children. The napkin on which Edna wrote the name they'd dreamed up was now framed and hanging on their office wall: *Hearts4Africa Home for Girls*. In slums, it was the girls who were at the greatest risk, so that's where they decided to begin.

Their first six-bed orphanage was as ramshackle as The New Boiling Soup Hotel. Their second was a condemned building.

Fifteen years on, Helen still found it hard to believe they'd turned what her father Ray had called 'Project Nuclear Bunker' into a light-filled home full of smiling girls. Most of them smiled, anyway. All had arrived traumatised. It took time. In some cases, days. In others, years.

It was Edna and Helen's firm belief that love was in the details. It was in Cook Rose's nutritious meals; in the tiny but well-stocked library; in the polished wood floors and the plum-hued bougainvillea spilling in at the windows.

In that first year, Helen's mum and dad had flown out from their home in the Scottish Highlands and spent two months camping in the grounds. Together with Edna's brother and cousin, they'd transformed two acres of rubble, litter and dirt into the flower-filled garden that it was today.

They'd flown out every other year since, so the grounds and orphanage were full of Scottish touches: tartan cushions on the worn sofas, lavender lining the paths. They'd taken Africa back to Scotland too. Rose had given Helen's mum Kenyan cooking lessons and Edna's cousin had taught Ray how to make wooden carvings.

Running Hearts4Africa involved a great deal of heartache but it also brought huge rewards. Two former orphans had recently graduated from the University of Nairobi. Yet Edna and Helen never forgot that for every orphan rescued, there were a hundred thousand waiting to be saved.

That's why tonight, as so often before, they went the extra mile.

'I'm worn out too,' said Edna, 'but I think we should search the streets around Mathare Valley one last time. The cholera outbreak is very worrying. What if we left behind a sick child whose life could have been saved if only we'd got to them in time?'

'But where is this child going to sleep?' asked Helen. 'We can't exactly put them in a tent in the garden. Wait! I've got it—'

'The library!' they said in unison and burst out

laughing. They'd been friends for so long they tended to finish each other's sentences.

'You're as bad as each other,' commented Tambo, Hearts4Africa's driver. 'No wonder the orphanage is overflowing.'

Helen paid no attention. 'We can string up that hammock someone donated. It'll be an unconventional bedroom but sort of romantic at the same time. The girl will sleep surrounded by stories. How about drawing straws to decide which of us breaks it to Matron? I'm not sure I'm brave enough.'

'I'll do it,' said Edna. 'Wanjiru doesn't scare me.'

The streets around Mathare were strewn with the wreckage left by the newly homeless. A spill of millet, a child's T-shirt, a three-legged chair.

'The police and developers who did this must

have calculators for hearts,' ranted Helen. 'How wicked would you have to be to want to destroy people who already have nothing? Where will their children sleep tonight? They have nowhere else to go.'

Edna glanced at her friend. She looked drained. It was a conversation they'd had many times. Edna knew that they'd keep on having it until wars stopped, droughts ended and governments became less corrupt.

'You're so good with our orphans, Helen. Do you still want children of your own some day? You used to talk about it all the time.'

'If I met the right person, I'd love children of my own, but that's not likely to happen. I'm thirty-eight and the years are slipping by faster and faster. As for adopting, we have so many orphans that if I chose one it wouldn't seem fair to the others.'

'In my experience, it's the other way around,' said Edna, who'd already adopted three of their orphans.

'Children choose you. It's a bit like falling in love. You look across a room and there's a connection. If they feel it too then you belong to one another.'

'You make it sound so easy.'

'Sometimes it is.'

Helen's phoned beeped. She checked the message and frowned.

'Everything okay?' asked Edna.

'I'm not sure. Mum hasn't been well and Dad sounds worried. That's not like him, as you know. If they spoke Swahili in Scotland, his middle name would be *Hakuna Matata*. Ray "No worries" Stuart.'

Edna knew exactly what she meant. One Christmas when Ray and Helen's mum had stayed at the orphanage, an Egyptian cobra had got into the pantry. Ray had calmly pressed its neck to the ground with a broom, picked it up and popped it into a sack. He'd released it on the outskirts of Nairobi.

The incident had become part of orphanage legend. Ray hadn't understood the fuss. 'Relatively speaking, cobras strike slowly. I was never in any danger.'

Edna, who loathed snakes, shuddered at the memory. 'If your mama is ill, will you have to return to Scotland?'

'It's hard to say. Mum is insisting that she'll be better in a few days but Dad has got me fretting. I'll give him a ring in the morning. Can you manage without me if I have to go to Scotland?'

'We could give Serena a chance to help run things. She's ready.'

Serena was one of their success stories. By the time she was eight she had lost both parents and a leg. Soon after starting Hearts4Africa, Helen and Edna had found her begging in the crime-ridden streets around Korogocho slum. Now she was an elegant twenty-three-year-old with a management diploma. The prosthetic blade on her left leg gave her a distinct advantage when she played football with the orphanage girls and staff.

'Good idea,' Helen said distractedly. 'Serena would be a real asset to us.'

She leaned forward and pointed. 'See there – up ahead. That's the Mercedes people have been telling us about. The one with no number plates. What possible reason could it have to be parked outside Mathare Valley at midnight, unless it's up to no good? Why don't you give your detective friend a ring, Edna? He might want to send someone to investigate.'

As she spoke, the Mercedes revved its engine and powered away, but Edna called the police anyway.

Helen squinted into the shadows as Tambo drove, afraid she might miss a sick or abandoned child. They'd found girls sheltering in unbelievable places – even bins.

Tambo braked sharply. 'What's going on there – on that street? That man – I think he's the Reaper.'

'The Reaper?'

'That simple giant we've been hearing about. The one criminals use for their dirty work.'

A hulk of a man was crouching beside a covered cart. When he stood he was over two metres tall. He bolted when he saw them, vaulting a wall with surprising agility.

Edna reported this development to the detective and ended the call. She too was exhausted. 'Guys, we've done as much as we can tonight. Let's get home to bed.'

The vehicle moved forward.

Helen rapped her window. 'Wait! Tambo, can you reverse a little? I think I saw something. A fox, maybe.'

Tambo snorted. 'There are no foxes in Nairobi unless they're on two legs. Must be a mongrel.

We can't afford any more pets at the orphanage. Already we are like a zoo with two dogs, three cats and a rabbit.'

Helen wasn't sure what she'd seen. It had resembled a fox, but that wasn't what caught her attention. It was the trail of sparks that had swirled behind it as it trotted out from under the cart. If it was a trick of the light, it was magical.

'I'm not about to adopt the fox or whatever it was, Tambo, but I do think we should take a closer look at that cart. What if the Reaper was about to harm something or someone?'

'Let's check it out,' agreed Edna. 'It'll only take a minute.'

They turned into the street. Tambo parked and left the engine running. As she climbed out, the night wind was cool on Helen's skin. She approached the cart cautiously, torch in hand. The fox had gone, but it could have left behind a wounded mate or cubs. She'd noticed a shimmer.

Kneeling, she lifted the tarpaulin. An emaciated girl with huge, terrified almond eyes cowered from the light. She was clutching a glass jar.

'Don't be afraid,' Helen said gently. 'I'm here to help you, not harm you. You're safe now.'

The girl's hand was freezing in hers. She'd sprained her ankle and couldn't walk. When Helen lifted her, she was nothing but bones. Despite that, Helen could feel the child's heart thrashing strongly against her cheek.

Edna came hurrying over to help. Tambo was guarding the vehicle. The area seemed deserted but appearances could be deceptive in and around the slums. The *Mungiki* used the drains and sewers as smugglers' tunnels. They could strip a vehicle of tyres, hubcaps and valuables and melt away in seconds.

Together, the women laid the girl on the blankets they'd prepared in the back of the 4x4. As soon as her head touched the pillow, she lost consciousness. It was as if she'd been holding on until she knew she could relax. Her hands relaxed and she let go of the jar.

Helen caught it before it smashed. Curiously, it was empty. A torn cardboard label was tied to it: 'FILL ME WITH SNOW'.

Helen looked from the jar to the girl and her entire world shifted on its axis.

'Would you mind calling the hospital, Edna?' she said weakly. 'Tell them we have a suspected case of cholera. They'll need to have all their wits about them. We have a life to save tonight.'

ONLY BOOKS HAVE
HAPPY ENDINGS

Even in her dreams, those Makena loved were always leaving. Those who wished to do her harm stayed. The *Mungiki* and the hyenas merged or took on one another's characteristics. The hyenas sported dreadlocks and brewed *chang'aa*; the *Mungiki* skulked through the woods with red eyes. They converged on her in nightmares, fangs bared.

At other times she was beneath the market cart, hiding her eyes as the Reaper reached under the tarpaulin. The Diplomat chased her in his Mercedes and once Priscilla offered her a platter piled high with raw meat.

Night after fevered night Makena ran from them, and as she ran she searched in vain for Mama, Baba and Snow.

'You'll never find them,' the Diplomat told her, leaning from his car window. 'They're a Tribe of Ghosts. Invisible.'

'You're lying,' Makena screamed at him. 'You have the wrong number.'

On the fourth afternoon, these dark dreams were interrupted by an overwhelming feeling of warmth and love. The hyenas were gone. She was underwater with Lucas, her mama's friend, who lived with fishes in his cool, green cave. 'I miss her so much,' she told him.

'So do I. But if they were here, your mama would tell you to keep on breathing, reading and climbing.

You'll get there in the end. Go on, breathe with me.'

'How can I?' Makena said. 'We're underwater in a cave. I'll get lost. I won't be able to find my way out.'

'All you have to do is look up. Kick hard. Swim towards the light.'

Makena awoke with a start. She was in a little library, surrounded by books. A woman was curled up in an armchair by the window, reading. The afternoon sun streamed in through the window, turning her tangled hair to flame. When she noticed Makena was conscious, she sat up so suddenly that her novel tumbled to the floor.

She smiled and said something in a British accent. Makena didn't catch it.

She came closer. 'I'm sorry about the hammock. We ran out of beds. Are you thirsty? You must be. Your temperature was through the roof. I'll get you some water.'

She started towards the door. Makena had a panic attack. She struggled upright in the hammock, pain spiking in her chest. 'Don't leave me! Don't leave me!'

The woman rushed to her side. Makena thought she heard her say: 'I'll never leave you. *Ninakupenda*. I'll be here for you always, I promise.' Then the fog swooshed in and Makena was powerless to resist it.

The nightmares were never as bad after that. The fox came more frequently and once Makena dreamed she was back at Tambuzi Rose Farm in the foothills of Mount Kenya. She and her mother were walking hand in hand through the packing shed. Makena found it odd to think that by morning, the roses would be on planes bound for the tables of princesses, pop stars or presidents in places as exotic as London and Mount Fuji, while she, a mere human, might never have the means to leave Kenya.

The roses had names like Ladykiller, Patience, Charity and Café Latte. Makena's favourite was Beatrice. Princess Charlene of Monaco had her own special rose, a ruffled confection of pink, salmon and apricot. Makena went from rose to rose, pressing her nose to their silky petals. Scents of jasmine, freshly picked apples, raspberry, vanilla and old-fashioned sweets filled her nostrils.

Her heart pinged like an elastic band. *Happy, happy, happy.*

When she stood up, Mama was gone and the shining fox was at her side. It spoke without words to her heart. 'I'll never leave you, Makena. *Ninakupenda.* I love you. I'll be here for you always, I promise.'

Six days later, Makena surfaced suddenly and completely. She blinked twice. The rainbow colours of the books flooded her vision. The fire-haired woman had gone from the chair by the window. In her place was an elegant young Kenyan, tapping a message into her phone.

'Where's the nurse?' Makena asked, her voice croaky from lack of use.

The woman jumped up. 'You're awake! I'm so glad. For a while there, we thought we'd lost you.' She came towards the hammock, smiling broadly.

Makena didn't smile back. 'Where is she?'

'You must mean Helen. She barely left your side after they found you. She even slept in that chair. She and Edna are the directors of Hearts4Africa. They're the ones who saved you – and me also, many years ago. They run this wonderful orphanage and now I do too. I'm Serena.'

'But where's Helen now?' Makena persisted. 'She said she would be here. Can you call her?'

Serena looked uncomfortable. 'I can't, honey. She's gone away.'

'When is she coming back?'

'She's not. Not for a long time. She had to return to Scotland. That's where she's from.'

A white-hot rage filled Makena. On a shelf between the books was her empty jam jar with its tatty label. Beside it were the photos of Mama and Baba, which someone had put in a frame. Like her parents and Snow, Helen had promised to be there always. Makena had heard her. Now she too had gone.

'The only happy endings are in books,' she said furiously. 'They don't happen in real life. It's all a big fat lie.'

Serena reached for her hand but Makena snatched it away and tucked it beneath the blanket. 'That's not true. This is a happy ending right here. You could have died, Makena. You had cholera. Thanks to Helen and

Edna, you have your whole life in front of you.'

Makena glared at her. 'You don't get it, do you? I don't want to be alive. They should have let me die.'

'You've been through a lot. So many of our girls feel the same when they arrive. Give us a chance. In time you will see—'

'If life is so full of happy endings, where is Snow?' demanded Makena. 'My friend, Snow, have you found her?'

'Helen said you talked about her in your sleep. The albino girl? We're concerned for her safety too. We've made some enquiries, but there's no news yet.'

'What about my mama and baba? Are you going to turn back the clock and bring them back to me?'

'No, but—'

'Is Helen here like she promised?'

'No, but—'

'Do you think someone will adopt me?'

'We will try to find you a family, of course. But after the age of four or five—'

'I know. Who would want a twelve-year-old, right?'

'It's harder but that doesn't mean—'

'Forget it,' said Makena. 'I don't want anyone. They'll only leave. That's what grown-ups do. They leave. Friends too. Everyone leaves.'

There was a long silence. Serena said tiredly: 'You should eat something, Makena. Can I get you some soup?'

Makena turned her face to the wall.

A LAND FIT FOR NOTHING
BUT POLAR BEARS

Inverness, Scotland. Six months later...

'Brace yourself, Makena. You're not in Africa now.'

Makena pulled her scarf over her face to hide a scowl. She knew very well that she was no longer in Africa. It had been blindingly obvious from the moment the Kenya Airways flight thudded on to the rain-drenched runway at Heathrow airport. Many hours later, another delayed, gale-tossed plane had deposited her in Inverness, Scotland, a place that made London look like a tropical paradise.

And here she was, being led out into a wind with the chill factor of the freezer her parents had owned in Nairobi. On hot days, Makena had loved to lean into it and sneak spoonfuls of her mama's homemade ice cream.

The memory brought burning tears to her eyes. Helen Stuart, who'd be fostering her for the next month, gave no sign of having noticed. It was probably just coincidence that she hugged Makena tighter as they fought their way across the dark car park to an ancient Jeep.

'Unfortunately, this old girl has only two temperatures – sub-Arctic or Saharan sizzler,' Helen said as she started the engine. 'Keep your jacket on until it's too hot to bear.'

The jacket, fleece and tartan scarf were new. So were the jeans. Gita, the Hearts4Africa volunteer who'd travelled with Makena as far as London before handing her over to a British Airways 'unaccompanied minor' flight attendant, had bundled her up in two cotton jumpers and leggings. Apparently, they were no defence against a Scottish winter. Helen had greeted Makena with a bag full of cold weather gear and insisted she change before they left the airport.

She looked older than Makena remembered, and whiter. Then again it was half a year since Makena had last seen her and back then she'd barely been conscious. Helen had sent her postcards of the Scottish Highlands, but Makena had barely glanced at them. From what she could tell, they were full of cheerful chitchat about the dire Scottish weather and sightings of birds and deer. There was nothing about why Helen had left so suddenly and never returned.

'Family troubles,' was all Edna would say.

She, Serena and Matron Wanjiru had become

Makena's surrogate mothers. They were all wonderful, even strict Matron, but Makena had not allowed herself to grow attached to any of them. Why would she? Even the best people made promises they couldn't keep.

'*We'll be back from Sierra Leone before you know it,*' her mama had said. '*You won't have time to miss us.*'

'*You're safe now,*' Helen told her. '*I'm going to take care of you. I'll never abandon you, I promise.*' Then she had.

Makena suspected that the orphanage director had only asked her to come to Scotland for Christmas because she felt guilty. She wasn't sure why she'd agreed to the visit. Perhaps because she was curious to see the place her father had talked of so often. She'd have to guard against getting close to Helen. If you didn't care about grown-ups, they couldn't hurt you. It was that straightforward.

The same applied to friends. One minute she and Snow had been as close as Siamese twins. Next, Snow had disappeared without trace. Edna and Serena had done everything they could to try to find her, but she'd vanished off the face of the earth. 'Presumed dead,' was what Makena had overheard a detective telling Edna.

'I can't believe I forgot gloves,' sighed Helen. She took Makena's dark brown hands and rubbed them briskly between her pale ones.

Embarrassed, Makena pulled away. 'I'm fine.'

'How about some hot chocolate?' Helen asked brightly, producing a flask. 'My grandmother's secret recipe. You can wrap your fingers around the cup. Stave off frostbite.'

Makena didn't answer but Helen poured her some anyway. Her hands trembled as she handed it over and Makena realised that she was nervous too. Even her voice was wobbly.

'It's so good to see you, Makena. Thanks for coming all this way. You must be exhausted. Once you've settled in and have caught up on sleep, I do hope you'll enjoy it. Nobody comes to Scotland for the weather, but it has other ways of stealing your heart.'

She took a deep breath. 'Right, let's get moving before we turn into ice statues.' Putting the Jeep into gear, she reversed.

A glimmer in the wing mirror caught Makena's eye. Something darted swift and low across the tarmac. Sparks spat behind it, like the tail of a shooting star.

'Stop!' yelled Makena.

Helen slammed on the brakes. Hot chocolate splattered against the windscreen and poured down Makena's front.

'Oh, my goodness. I'm so sorry. Are you burned?' Frantically, Helen swabbed her down with tissues.

'I'm okay, I'm okay.' Makena snatched the box and mopped her dripping jacket herself. She'd been in Scotland less than an hour and already it was a disaster. She should never have come.

'My new clothes are ruined and it's all my fault,' she burst out.

But Helen wasn't upset or cross. She was smiling. 'Don't be daft. I'll pop everything into the washing machine and it'll be clean and dry by morning. It's really my fault for not bringing you a cup with a lid. Besides, you saved us from having an accident. What did I nearly hit?'

She twisted round to scan the empty car park. 'What did you see?'

'I'm not sure.' Makena was reluctant to admit that her mind had likely been playing tricks on her. 'I saw something. I definitely saw something.'

SILENT NIGHT

Makena had spent much of the flight trying to picture Helen's home and was convinced she'd know it by sight. At the orphanage, Helen's room had been furnished with a single bed, a plain rug, one picture, a Bible and a few dog-eared novels. Makena had caught a peek of it on the day Serena moved into it and had been surprised that the co-director of Hearts4Africa had lived so humbly and in one room. Edna, the other director, lived in a cottage in the grounds, but then she had a husband and three children.

However, everyone knew that in the UK things were different. It wasn't that Makena imagined that all British people lived in castles and stately homes. But Helen's Scottish house would, Makena felt sure, be large.

She had an idea that it would be painted cream and have a long curving driveway and columns framing a forest-green front door. There was bound to be a library. Helen, she'd been told, loved books as much as she did. The kitchen would be hung with hams (Makena tried not to think about the hams or the haggis) and bulbs of garlic. The living room would be tidy and decorated with antiques and velvet armchairs. She and Helen would drink tea and eat cream scones in front of a crackling fire.

On the way out of Inverness she actually glimpsed such a house, its windows cheerfully lit. But Helen drove past it and on into the night. Suburbs and one-shop villages gave way to lonely landscapes of unremitting bleakness.

The roads emptied and for a while they saw nothing and no one. Then two lorries screamed over a rise, the gale of their passing almost blowing the Jeep off the road. The cab of the first lorry was briefly illuminated. The driver hunched over the wheel, jowls taut with concentration.

Is he a man or a Tokoloshe? Makena wondered. From what she could tell, Scotland appeared a great deal more suited to water-sprites with dark impulses than sunny Africa. She pictured them lurking under bridges with trolls. Coaxed out by drivers desperate to stay awake, the bad fairies would take the wheel of lorries bound for distant cities. Later, they'd demand payment in chocolate and haggis.

Thinking about the Tokoloshe reminded her of the drive to Nanyuki with her mama and Uncle Samson. She'd been so innocent then. Secure in her parents' love, the future had seemed as limitless as the blue sky arching overhead.

She remembered bouncing in the backseat (she was always bouncing in those days), brimming over at the thought of the mountain adventure to come. It had annoyed her that her mother wanted to take a detour to the rose farm. *'You're always in such a hurry, Makena... If all you do is run, run, run, you can miss what is right in front of you.'*

She'd been right. Makena had been so busy obsessing about the days ahead that she'd hardly been able to focus on anything else. If her mama had been a different sort of person, they might have driven past Tambuzi without turning their heads. They'd never have stopped to smell the roses.

Days later, her mama and her baba were gone for ever and not so long after that she'd been at the mercy of Priscilla.

As soon as she'd got her strength back at the Home for Girls, she'd called her uncle. Serena had given her permission to use the orphanage phone.

Throughout her month in the slum, Makena had felt a nagging sense of guilt. It had been wrong of her to persuade the lorry driver to drop her off at her old house, and unforgivable that she hadn't contacted Uncle Edwin to say that she hadn't felt able to go to the Tings.

Once he discovered that his niece had never arrived at her friends' home, Edwin was sure to have called the police. For all she knew, detectives had been combing Nairobi for months, trying to trace her. Priscilla could have repented of her actions within hours of Makena leaving. She and Edwin might have been in despair ever since, fearing the worst.

When she'd finally called, Edwin had answered on the first ring. The baby was crying in the background.

'Ah, Makena, it's you,' he said without enthusiasm. 'Sorry I haven't been in touch but you won't believe what's happened since you left. I have been through hell.'

Makena immediately leaped to the worst conclusions. One of the children had a terminal illness. Edwin had been fired and the family was destitute and out on the streets. Priscilla had abandoned the children and run off with her secret friend. *Edwin* had a terminal illness.

Her uncle said hoarsely: 'Priscilla has left us – me and the kids. She's taken up with a rich lawyer. He's divorced; a terrible man. Everyone knows that he beat his last wife. Because I have wronged her, Priscilla is not seeing straight. When she does, she will come home. We miss her. We are not coping on our own.'

'I'm sorry, Uncle,' said Makena. And she was.

The baby squalled louder. Her uncle carried the phone to the pram. He squeaked a toy and jingled a bell.

Makena held the receiver away from her ear. When the baby calmed, he came back on the line. He sounded stressed.

'How are things, Makena? The lorry driver told me you're in a great home. He said that when he dropped you off, the man who came to greet you was dressed like a rich politician. He told me the lawn was like the putting green at a golf club.'

'Yes, I'm very fortunate,' said Makena, and she was. Fortunate to be in Hearts4Africa's caring Home for Girls. *She'd* been rescued from the streets. Countless others hadn't.

'Any day now, Priscilla will be home,' Edwin was mumbling. 'Perhaps it's better if you don't call here, Makena. Not for a while. I don't want her frightened away again. If you need me, you can always leave a message at the garage.'

'Bye, Uncle Edwin.'

239

'Go well, niece.'

Makena hung up. She felt as empty as a fallen dove's egg, its shell pecked clean by crows.

The drive to Helen's home seemed interminable. The Jeep groaned up hills and creaked round hairpin bends. Makena was aching with weariness when at last a mountain road led them to a five-barred gate. Beyond it was a dark stone cottage. In the glare of the headlights, the smoke from the chimney zig-zagged in the fierce wind. A creaking sign was painted with the words: 'The Great Escape'.

'My mum came up with the name,' Helen said with a laugh. 'She and Dad spent decades doing dull, safe jobs in London before they had an epiphany – a revelation. They decided that what they wanted more than anything was to live in nature, surrounded by mountains, doing jobs they loved. So they packed up pretty much overnight and ... escaped.'

She jumped out to open the gate, letting in an icy gust. When she climbed back into the Jeep her face was serious.

'Makena, I should tell you that my mum passed away at the end of June. That's why I had to leave the orphanage – and you – and come rushing back to Scotland. Dad's not been the same since. The shock of Mum's death brought on a mild stroke and he's lost the ability to speak. Doctors say there's no medical reason for it. Whatever the cause, he doesn't talk. Doesn't do much of anything if I'm honest. All I'm saying is, don't take it personally.'

She smiled but her eyes were sad. 'And on that note, welcome to The Great Escape.'

The hallway had been designed for dwarves. Helen had to duck as they entered. But the cottage seemed to expand as they went. The kitchen was enormous. A welcome wave of warmth enveloped Makena as they walked in. The source of the heat was the Aga, an old-fashioned oven, which, like the cabinets, was a spirit-lifting blue. An oak table was laid for dinner with a cracker beside each plate.

The kitchen opened out on to a glass room called a conservatory. It was a friendly space decorated with a squashy sofa, a coffee table piled with books and a Persian rug. It was too dark to see the view outside but that didn't matter because Makena only had eyes for one thing: the Christmas tree sparkling in the corner.

It was a chunky tree with attitude. Its bristly arms supported reindeers, bears in Santa hats and any number of red, gold and silver balls. Stars twirled and winked. As Makena moved closer, the smell of wood and pine needles transported her straight to Mount Kenya. She gasped with delight.

'It's a Norway spruce,' said Helen. 'I was planning a bog-standard balsam fir but it was love at first sight. There's only one thing missing and that's the angel at the top. I thought I might leave that for you to put on.'

Her words were a dash of cold water in Makena's face. She had no right to be happy. How could she be happy when her parents were dead and her best friend had met some unknown fate?

'I don't believe in angels,' she snapped. Then she marched to the door and picked up her suitcase. 'Where should I put this?'

If Helen was crushed, she hid it well. 'I'll show you to your room shortly. First, if you don't mind, I'd like you to meet my father.'

In the living room, the fire was dying. The television screen was a hissing grey fuzz. Helen turned on a lamp. A ghost of a man slumped in an armchair, staring blankly at the screen. He barely registered their presence.

Helen started forward. 'Oh, Dad, why have you been sitting in the dark again? And I've told you a hundred times that if you press the DVD button on the remote, it all goes to pot.'

Exasperated, she turned off the TV. 'Dad, this is Makena, who'll be joining us for Christmas and most of January. You have loads in common so I'm sure you'll get along famously. Makena's father was a mountain guide too. He led dozens of expeditions up Mount Kenya. Makena, meet Ray.'

Makena approached shyly. She extended a nervous hand.

Ray's grey eyes swept over her unseeingly. When his fingers touched hers, they were as cold and bony as a skeleton's. It was all Makena could do to keep from screaming.

'Who's hungry?' asked Helen with fake cheer. 'Makena, Dad, would you like some soup and nibbles?'

Her father shook his head without enthusiasm.

The plane food had been inedible and Makena was starving, but the thought that she might be presented with cow's stomach lining stuffed with sheep's heart, liver, lungs and oatmeal was not appealing.

'I don't need anything. Thanks,' she added, remembering her manners. 'Please, I'm very tired. Is it all right if I go to bed now?'

Helen opened her mouth then shut it again firmly. As she led the way up the stairs, Makena heard her mutter: 'At this rate, Christmas really will be a silent night.'

LIONS, FOXES AND BEARS

At Hearts4Africa's Home for Girls, Makena's nightmares had ceased soon after the Reaper and Diplomat were arrested. Turned out, the Diplomat was not an attaché to a foreign embassy at all. He was a greedy local businessman in league with the Mungiki mafia. He paid a pittance to the Reaper, whose real name was Demetrios, to trawl the slums for stray children fit enough to work in his sportswear factory. In exchange for what one boy claimed was rat stew, and lodgings not fit for cattle, they had to work around the clock making trainers and polo shirts.

According to Serena, Demetrios himself had been abandoned as a baby. The sailor who found him on the docks in Mombasa had named him Demetrios because the last ship to leave the port was returning to Athens. It was the only Greek name he knew.

'The Reaper's Greek?' marvelled Makena, recalling the giant as she'd seen him in the storm. He'd reared out of the driving rain like Zeus, the dark god of thunder and lightning.

Once she knew his history, her nightmares about Demetrios stopped, perhaps because she no longer saw him as a monster but as another of Mathare Valley's tragic stories. During her last month in the orphanage, she'd slept the fathomless sleep of the world-weary in her hammock in the library.

For that reason, it was particularly distressing

that on her first night in The Not-so-Great Escape, she had a new nightmare.

In it, her parents were alive but just out of reach. Whenever she tried to touch them, they evaporated like mist.

'Try harder, Makena,' her mama kept saying. 'Come closer so I can hug you. I miss you so much.'

Makena brushed away tears and sat up in bed. She hated Scotland already. It was fit only for polar bears. Fancy Helen thinking Makena would have anything in common with her creepy dad – apart, that is, from him being a mountain guide like Baba. That was a weird coincidence. Other than that, she was a stranger in a strange house. The thought of being stuck in the middle of nowhere with Helen and Ray for weeks on end was too horrible for words. And yet what choice did she have?

Would she ever again find a place she could call home?

Secretly, she'd been looking forward to seeing Scotland. In a strange way, she thought it might make her feel nearer to Baba. He'd adored his Scottish clients and had always spoken of the Highlands as being uncannily like the heather zone of Mount Kenya. So far Makena had only viewed the landscape through a rain-splattered windscreen and in the white semi-circle of headlights, but she wasn't seeing any resemblance. She'd expected snow, for one thing, but from what she could see it was just fold after fold of pewter-grey mountains and hills.

She was having the same trouble with Helen. Now that she knew that the orphanage director had left Nairobi to be with her dying mother, she felt bad that she'd resented her for doing what was right and going to be with her family. It's just that Makena didn't have a family. She'd needed Helen too.

Thinking about it now, she wasn't sure why.

The weeks of her illness were so hazy she barely remembered the woman. What she did recall was the feeling of her. An intense warmth. In the months that followed Makena had swung between hating Helen for saving her and feeling a certain kinship with her.

At night, away from the eyes of the other orphans, she'd read books she'd been told were Helen's favourites: *Little Women* and *The Lion, the Witch and the Wardrobe*. She'd found herself listening whenever anyone talked about the scrapes Helen and Edna had got into as directors of Hearts4Africa – some funny, some deadly. They'd routinely risked their lives standing up to corrupt officials, armed gangsters and evil slum landlords as they travelled Kenya's no-go areas helping children. Serena idolised them both.

'If it weren't for Edna and Helen I wouldn't be here now. They did more than simply save my life.

They saw beyond the dirt and my missing leg to the person inside. They made me believe I was worth saving. Now I have a management diploma and can help my community as I have been helped.'

In photos, Helen always seemed to be laughing. Her wildfire hair was cut in an unruly bob, as if she'd been called away to help a child in mid-haircut.

When she'd been told that Helen had invited her to the Scottish Highlands for Christmas, Makena had veered between being resentful because she was sure that Helen had asked her to Scotland for all the wrong reasons, and being quietly thrilled that, of all the girls in the orphanage, she was the one Helen had chosen to foster for a month.

But the smiling Helen of the orphanage photos and the one who'd met her at the airport were not the same at all. Scottish Helen was dull in both looks and spirit. Her spark had gone. The harder she tried to be relaxed and friendly, the more anxious she seemed.

Makena knew better than anyone how shattering it was to lose a parent. How one minute you were upright and full of plans and next you were buried alive under the rubble of your ruined life. Even if you managed to crawl out, an invisible knife stayed stuck in your chest and twisted randomly. At times you could hardly breathe for the pain.

However, Helen had a home. She also had a father. It wasn't the same as being alone in the world, thousands of miles from your own country.

Even allowing for his recent bereavement, Ray did not match the Ray of orphanage legend either. Nairobi Ray had chopped logs, laid floors, built walls and created a garden from a rubbish heap with his bare hands. He'd subdued a cobra and insisted on releasing it into the wild. Scottish Ray did not look capable of facing down a Mount Kenya mole shrew, much less guiding people up mountains. Makena wondered if the tales about him had been exaggerated.

She also wondered about her air ticket. Perhaps it could be changed. She could tell Helen that she was homesick for Africa and wanted to return on the next plane. Whatever her issues, Helen had a kind heart. She could hardly refuse.

The clock on Makena's bedside table said two-fifteen a.m. but she couldn't sleep. It wasn't that the bed was uncomfortable. The duvet was as fluffy as the clouds that floated halfway up Mount Kenya, too idle to climb any higher.

As for the mattress, after the sofa with the stabbing springs at her uncle's house, the smelly, shared cardboard in the slum and the orphanage hammock, let's just say that the Scottish bed did not go unappreciated.

Unfortunately, the bed was in Scotland, a country Makena intended to leave as soon as possible. She had no doubt that Helen had gone to great lengths to make her room in the eaves welcoming. The bookcase took up one whole wall. It was a treasure trove. Helen had told her to help herself to anything she wanted. It was a pity that Makena wouldn't be around to take her up on the offer.

There was a wooden giraffe that watched her from the corner and a drawing pad and pencil case on a small desk. Above it, was a painting of herds of giraffe and zebra grazing on a plain, with a snow-capped Mount Kenya in the distance. Only two things in the room belonged to Makena: the photos of her parents, and Snow's empty jam jar with its crumpled label. She'd put them on her bedside table in an attempt to make herself feel more at home.

Makena fumbled for the lamp. If she was

planning to leave after breakfast, she might as well get ready now. Unable to find the switch, she pushed up the blind to let in some moonlight.

It was snowing! Flakes drifted past the window like white rose petals. Billowy piles collected in the garden.

Entranced by the wonderland below, she pulled the duvet round her shoulders and leaned on the sill. The ordinary had become extraordinary. Threadbare trees wore snow leopard cloaks. Bushes and shrubs had become a parade of white lions, tigers and bears. The mountain was a Christmas cake, its crags iced with white.

She wanted to race downstairs, twirl in it and even roll in it. She wanted to lose herself in the magic of it.

A movement caught her eye. There was a figure out in the snow. To her astonishment it was Ray. He was carrying something.

With a spryness that belied his thin frame, he crossed the garden to a shed. He disappeared inside. Long minutes ticked by. Makena began to worry. It was freezing and Ray was in his pyjamas and dressing gown. She wondered if she should wake Helen. Clearly he was losing his marbles. If he couldn't operate a television remote, he should not be out in the snow in the dead of night.

She was trying to pluck up the courage to call Helen when Ray emerged, holding the shed door open as if waiting for someone to follow. Makena pressed her face to the cold glass. Small creatures spilled out into the snow. She strained her eyes to make them out. Were they puppies?

Ray set his torch on a garden bench and sat down. Four scraps of ginger fur came barrelling into the light. Fox cubs.

The memory of the bat-eared fox with water

diamonds in its whiskers came back to Makena with crystal clarity. These were different but just as adorable. They tore in circles, dodging shadows and snapping at snowflakes. Ray leaned down and they nibbled his fingers.

At length, he attempted to scoop them up. They scampered out of range, enjoying the game. It was some time before he was able to coax them back into the shed.

Makena waited for Ray to return to the cottage. He was in his slippers. His toes must have been frozen solid. But he stayed where he was. Switching off his torch, he gazed up at the mountain. Feathery flakes fell faster and faster, settling on his head and the shoulders of his dressing gown.

Then something even odder happened. A silver fox appeared at his side. It had an unusually bushy tail with a starlight shimmer. Ray didn't look round or

react to the creature in any way. The two of them just stood together, staring up at the snowy peaks.

Makena watched until her eyes began to close on their own. She lay down. Seconds later, she was fast asleep.

THE GO-BETWEEN

She awoke after nine, so famished she could have gnawed her own arm off. Helen had breakfast ready. Porridge was one of Makena's least favourite things (along with Eunice's potluck gruel in Mathare Valley) but Helen topped it with apples stewed in cinnamon and a dash of maple syrup and it was delicious.

They ate in the warm kitchen. It was a brilliant blue morning and the sight of the mountains, white with creases of granite showing through, filled Makena's chest with a feeling so strong it made her dizzy.

Her father had always told her that mountain air was in her blood. He and her mama had hiked to Point Lenana when Makena was still in the womb, and had often joked that Mount Kenya was in her DNA. Her earliest memory was watching her father return from a climbing trip with his coiled ropes slung round his shoulder and crampons, ice axes and other technical gear hung from, or stuffed into, his backpack. She'd taken it for granted that when she grew up she'd be a mountain guide like him.

But that dream was long gone. These days, her grandest ambition was getting through the next twenty-four hours. She did not see mountains in her future. If she had a future. Yet when she stared out at the sharp white ridge, its teeth biting into the clear sky, she couldn't help but feel that familiar pull.

Helen came over with a glass of orange juice just as Makena was working up to her speech about hating

Scotland and wanting to go back to Africa on the next plane.

'A pair of sleepyheads, you and my father are, Makena. I'm glad. I'm sure you needed it after your epic journey. I might check on Dad, though. He's always been one of those annoying early risers; as perky at four a.m. in a snowstorm as the average person is at ten in summer. Since Mum died, he's been lying in a lot more. Some days I get the feeling he can't be bothered to get up. But nine-thirty is late even by his new standards.'

She reappeared in a hurry, phone in hand. 'He's burning up. I'm calling the doctor. I think he has a fever.'

It all came back to Makena then, Ray and the five foxes. The four playful youngsters and the regal silver one. She'd wondered if she'd dreamed the whole thing. What if Ray had caught pneumonia, hanging out in the snow in his PJs?

Makena was in an agony of indecision. Should she say anything or not? She decided against it. For some reason it felt disloyal.

As soon as breakfast was over, Helen began preparing some minestrone soup for her father. 'Another recipe of my grandmother's. Best tonic I know. If this doesn't cure him, I don't know what will.'

'Would it be okay if I go out to see the snow?' Makena asked shyly. If she was to leave Scotland soon, she wanted to fill Snow's jar. Then she'd have honoured her promise to her friend.

'Of course! But are you sure you don't want to wait until I can come with you? I was so looking forward to sharing it with you.'

Makena didn't answer. Snow was sacred. It was the bond between her and Baba and her best friend. When she touched it for the first time, she wanted to be alone.

A flicker of hurt flashed across Helen's face, but she covered it with a smile. 'Wrap up warm, honey, and stay where I can see you, in front of the conservatory window.'

Makena had imagined snow for so long that its rice crispy crunch and the way it swallowed her boots came as no surprise. But the pearly sparkle of it did. She kneeled in it, not caring that it soaked through her jeans. She made a snowball, packing it tight and juggling it from hand to cold hand.

Hot tears came into her eyes. In Nairobi, she'd wished so much that the snow in her jar had stayed as frozen and pristine as it had been on the peak of Batian. Now she'd have done anything to have her old jar of melted snow, turning slightly green, if it meant her mama and baba were still alive, still loving her.

There was a knock at the conservatory window. 'Makena, won't you come inside now before I have two invalids on my hands? I've made you a cup of hot chocolate. With marshmallows on top!'

Makena saw that the snow in her hands was melting between her fingers. She got to her feet, feeling a thousand years old. She realised that she'd forgotten to bring the jam jar down from her room. Before she left Scotland, she'd have to find time to fill it up.

Ray's condition worsened rapidly. Helen played it down but was clearly alarmed. Dr Brodie, a man with a red beard abundant enough to house a family of mice, came and went at regular intervals. He'd diagnosed bronchitis. Hospital was mentioned but Ray refused to consider it.

Curled up by the fire with a mystery novel, Makena couldn't help overhearing the heated debate. The doctor's broad Scottish accent boomed down the stairs.

'The bad news is, he's more stubborn than an arthritic mule. On the plus side, he has years of healthy living behind him. At the peak of his guiding career, he was the fittest man I'd ever met. Muscles like granite. Lungs like a dolphin. Keep feeding him nettle tea and minestrone soup and he'll get through it.'

That night, Makena couldn't sleep. She kept thinking about Ray and how he was ill because he'd been playing with the orphaned foxes in the snow. Had he also been taking them food? If so, wouldn't they be ravenous by now?

Makena jumped out of bed and pulled on all the winter clothes she possessed. Thanks to Helen, there were a lot. She crept downstairs. In the kitchen, she paused and listened. Not a peep. She opened the fridge. What did fox cubs eat? More importantly, what could she take that wouldn't be missed?

In the end, she tore up four slices of bread and

put the pieces in a bowl with a few raw eggs. It looked disgusting but then she wasn't a fox.

Getting out of the cottage was the scariest part. When she opened the back door, she was as nervous as a burglar on the brink of cracking a safe. If it was alarmed, she'd be in trouble.

It turned out it wasn't even locked. 'Not a lot of crime in these parts,' Helen had told her. Remembering the lawlessness of Mathare, Makena couldn't understand how she'd coped.

Makena set off across the snowy garden, clutching the torch she'd found on a shelf in the hallway. With every step she expected to hear a shout, but the cottage stayed dark.

Only when she reached the shed did she dare turn on the torch. Four terrified ginger faces peered up at her from a nest of blankets. She'd worried that they'd refuse to take food from a stranger, but they

were too famished to care. They yapped with delight when she set the bowl down. Makena sat and watched them eat till their bellies were bursting.

Something kindled inside her, a forgotten feeling of joy. Before it could take hold she stood abruptly. As she hurried to the cottage, hoping that the falling snow would conceal her footsteps, she noticed Ray's curtains move. She squinted up at the window but saw nothing further.

In the kitchen, she washed and dried the bowl before tiptoeing back to bed. It was a while before she could sleep. She was far from Kenya, in one of the coldest places on earth, but all of a sudden her heart felt warm.

A JAR OF SNOW

From then on, Makena routinely crept out between midnight and dawn. She grew bold enough to play with the cubs in the snow, but was careful to erase all traces afterwards. Never once did she see the silver fox with the magnificent tail.

In the lead-up to Christmas, Helen went out of her way to ensure that Makena did not feel forgotten during the crisis with her father. When she wasn't preparing broths or hot water bottles, she and Makena made gingerbread bears together, watched *The Wizard of Oz* and went on walks.

271

Makena had decided to put off asking to fly back to Kenya until Ray was better. It didn't seem fair to add to Helen's burden at such a difficult time.

Makena was surprised at how rapidly her own fitness returned. At her parents' home in Nairobi, she'd worked hard at it, shinning up and down her climbing wall, running at school and playing tennis with her mama with the aim of one day being strong enough to scale mountains.

Strolling through a snowy forest one afternoon with Helen, Makena was struck by the realisation that the elephant had gone from her chest. It seemed to have been left behind in Mathare Valley. After the crowded clamour of the slum, the pure, gushing mountain streams and silence and space of the Scottish Highlands was a luxury she was still getting used to.

When they emerged from the trees an hour later,

the low dark sky had the look of a smouldering ember. They were crossing a field of fresh snow when the winter sun pierced the clouds. The white landscape came to sparkling life, as if lit by laser beams. Makena stopped. She unzipped a side pocket in her new rucksack and took out the empty jam jar.

Without ceremony, she filled it with snow. There was no fuss, no song and dance. It just felt like the right moment to do it. As she put on the lid, she sent up a prayer that wherever Snow was, whether in this world or the next, she was dancing.

Helen watched without comment. When they resumed their walk, she took Makena's hand. Makena was tempted to pull away but didn't want to hurt her feelings. After a while, she found she quite liked it.

'Would you believe that, in the autumn, this entire area is carpeted in purple heather,' Helen was saying. 'When Dad and I went hiking on Mount

273

Kenya, we couldn't get over how similar the East African moorland was to ours. We stayed in these log cabins called Rutundu on a gorgeous loch. That's the place where Prince William proposed to Kate.'

'I know about the log cabins!' Makena cried, forgetting her rule about not discussing her parents with Helen or anyone else. 'Me and Baba camped near Rutundu. On the banks of the River Kathita.'

Helen's face was aglow, the way it had been in the orphanage photos. 'Did you hear the hyenas laughing at night? It was so eerie I couldn't sleep.'

'Neither could I. I had a nightmare.'

'I was a nervous wreck too,' laughed Helen. 'I kept imagining hyenas converging on the cabins in packs. Dad reminded me that, like vultures, they prefer carrion – you know, decaying flesh – but I wasn't convinced. Did you see the trout in Lake Rutundu? They're as big as beluga whales.'

Caught up in the moment, Makena heard herself say: 'I saw a bat-eared fox on the shore of Lake Rutundu. It was drinking and when it looked up there were water diamonds in its whiskers. When I told Baba he said there was no such thing as foxes on Mount Kenya, but I think he believed me in the end.'

Helen was unfazed. 'Foxes turn up in all sorts of unlikely places. In London, they're in every suburban garden. Once, a couple walked into a restaurant near Piccadilly Circus. Funnily enough, I thought I saw a fox the night Edna and I found you in Nairobi. We were about to move on when it caught my eye. Apparently, there are no foxes in Nairobi so I must have been mistaken, but I did see something. Whatever it was left a trail of sparks. A trick of the light, I suppose, but it was enchanting.'

'A trail of sparks?'

275

The ground rolled under Makena's feet. She recalled the creature she'd glimpsed in the airport car park, trailing sparks like hot ash.

'Yes. If it hadn't been for that, we might have driven on without checking under the market cart. When I think we might never have found you, I get heart palpitations.'

She stopped. 'Are you feeling faint, Makena? You seem a little wobbly. Maybe we've been out too long. It's bitingly cold.'

'We can't both be wrong,' said Makena, recovering. 'About the foxes, I mean. Either we're both right or both wrong. Or one of us is right and the other is wrong.'

'There's another explanation too.'

'Which is?'

'That we both have an over-active imagination,' Helen said with a smile. 'Although, personally, I think that's something to be encouraged. There's an Einstein quote I love. "Logic will get you from A to Z. Imagination will get you everywhere." He called it a "preview of life's coming attractions".'

Her eyes met Makena's and dropped away awkwardly as each became aware that they were having a mother–daughter moment.

Helen hastily changed the subject. 'See the church steeple in the valley between those hills, and the dark dots beside it? That's the local school. Some of the kids ride to lessons on horses. In PE, they do regular sports such as football and hockey, but they also learn kayaking, climbing and skiing.'

'There's a school similar to that near Mount Kenya,' Makena told her. 'It's right on the Equator. There are pupils who have breakfast at home in the Southern Hemisphere and lunch at school in the Northern Hemisphere. It's really cool.'

It was a school she'd always wished she could attend and it was comforting to learn that, half a world away, Scottish children also liked wilderness adventures. She admitted to Helen that she'd half expected them to be too busy playing video games and watching television to care much about nature.

'Some Scottish kids do prefer TV and technology to the great outdoors,' said Helen. 'I think that's true of kids all over these days. But in my experience, the children of the Highlands understand that while those things are fun, the best adventures are found in the wild.'

'Was that your school — the one in the valley?' Makena asked.

'Sadly not. Mine was on a polluted London road with a concrete playground. I was eighteen when Mum and Dad moved to Scotland and not ready to leave the bright lights. I did my degree in London then took a gap year to volunteer in Kenya. I fell in love with the country and its people but not with the charity. Edna and I were young, fired-up and idealistic. We decided we could do a far better job on our own. Sometimes we have; at other times it's been a disaster, but I don't regret a single hour. Hearts4Africa has, in a sense, been the love of my life.

'Things have changed, though. For the foreseeable future, my life is here. I'm not concerned about Hearts4Africa. Edna and Serena will do a marvellous job without me and I can help by fundraising in the UK. But I pine for Africa, as I'm sure you do. It's in my blood. Until Mum passed away, I'd spent more time in Kenya than I had in Scotland.'

She stared up at the forbidding mountain. 'This is new for me too.'

NO ANGEL

On Christmas Eve, Makena came downstairs to find Ray sitting on the sofa beneath a pile of blankets. He was eating Marmite toast and watching a documentary about penguins in the Antarctic. Though as gaunt and grizzled as a scarecrow, he had more colour in his cheeks.

A smile flitted across his lips when he saw Makena. He seemed on the verge of speaking, but Helen walked in and he turned his attention to the screen.

That day was one of the loveliest Makena could remember. A friend of Ray's came to keep an eye on him for a few hours and she and Helen went to the Glencoe Café near Loch Leven. There was a life-sized reindeer made of willow on the doorstep. Makena ordered a hot chocolate topped with whipped cream and pink marshmallows. The waitress who brought it was wearing a Santa hat.

The main street bustled with thirty or so people doing last-minute shopping. Helen described it as 'packed'. For the first few days in Scotland Makena had wondered where everyone was. The Highlands seemed virtually uninhabited. Then she figured it out. The perishing cold discouraged visitors.

Makena found Glencoe charming but not nearly as interesting as *The Three Sisters, Devil's Staircase* and *Buachaille Etive Mor* and *Buachaille Etive Beag.* Those were the mountains that gave Glencoe its frontier-town atmosphere.

Ben Nevis, Britain's tallest mountain, was only one thousand three hundred and forty-six metres, less than a third of the size of Mount Kenya. But what the mountains of Scotland lacked in height, they made up for in wind-blasted ruggedness. The wildness of the crags and clouds that sent dragon-shadows swooping across the village set Makena's skin tingling. She was forced to revise her opinion of Ray. If he'd been a guide here, he must once have been tough.

That afternoon, she helped Helen bake mince pies. They ate them warm and smothered with cream in front of the fire. Somehow the fact that the wind was howling outside made them extra scrumptious.

When night drew in, Helen and Makena took turns at reading *The Velveteen Rabbit* out loud. Ray had recovered enough to sit whittling away at a block of wood with a small knife. Gradually, a pair of pointy ears emerged. Makena was startled to realise that he was the artist behind the exquisite animal carvings dotted around the cottage.

'First time I've seen him work with wood since Mum died,' confided Helen, relief mingling with sorrow in her voice.

Worryingly, Ray was still weak and coughing. They looked up from a passage in the book to find he'd slipped off to bed. Makena was weary too. The fox cubs were divine but the lack of sleep was catching up with her.

Before going up to her room, she went into the kitchen to get a glass of water. The Christmas tree twinkled contentedly in the conservatory. Makena wished her mama could have been there to see it. She'd always adored Christmas. The spruce's luxuriant lower branches curled around a pile of presents tied with gold, pink and red ribbons and bows.

Guilt thwacked her over the head. What was

wrong with her? Was she so faithless that she'd already forgotten that her parents, Aunt Mary and her best friend were gone and did not have the luxury of enjoying Christmas?

She glared at the tree. It was still missing an angel.

THE LETTER

The ticking of the radiator as it warmed her room in the eaves woke Makena. She stretched lazily. When she remembered it was Christmas Day, her heart did a little skip. She forgot to feel bad about her good fortune and allowed herself to dream about the presents and promised roast that lay ahead. There was even veggie haggis. Helen and Ray were both vegetarians and her dietary choice had never been an issue.

Then she caught sight of the clock. It was seven-twelve a.m. She'd forgotten to set the alarm so she

285

could feed the foxes! It was doubtful that Ray had been well enough to tend to them, which meant they would have gone hungry.

Makena flew out of bed and wriggled into her jeans, thermal vest, fleece and jacket. She shoved her gloves into her pocket and pulled a woolly hat over her braids. A week before she'd left Nairobi, Gloria's daughter had turned up at the Hearts4Africa Home for Girls. Nadira was training to be a hairdresser herself and came often, Serena said, to hone her skills on the orphans. Her sessions were wildly popular and girls queued up to be one of her models.

Makena was self-conscious about her hair and did not join the queue, but Edna came to fetch her and told her she had her own private appointment with Nadira. When Makena asked why, Edna gave the enigmatic, all-purpose answer of grown-ups across the globe: 'Because I said so.'

Nadira never asked how Makena had ended up at the orphanage and Makena never told her. Nor did she comment on the state of Makena's hair.

All she said was: 'I hear you're on your way to the UK for Christmas. We need to sharpen up your look. It's about time someone showed those Brits, with their dragged-through-a-thorn-bush-backwards   hair-dos that we Kenyan ladies can teach them a thing or two about style.'

Down in the kitchen, Makena considered the cubs' dining options. The bread was almost gone. So were the eggs. As she deliberated over the mince pies, she spotted Helen's laptop on the kitchen bench. It would only take a minute to do a Google search on whether raisins and piecrust would make the fox cubs sick. Helen would never know.

Hopping on to a stool, she tapped a key. The screen flared to life. An email popped up. Makena

was about to sweep it aside when she saw the address:
glasgowadoptionservices@globalmail.com.

A cold feeling came over her. It was dated the
twenty-fourth of December and marked 'URGENT!'
She knew it was private but she had to read it.

Helen Stuart <helen.stuart73@gmail.com>
to Glasgowadoptionservices@globalmail.com ▾

Dear Mr Carrick,
Thank you for helping to organise documentation for
Makena Wambora, the twelve-year-old Kenyan girl
I am fostering for Christmas. I beg your assistance
again on a matter of the greatest urgency.

As soon as Makena stepped off the plane, I knew
I'd made a terrible mistake. I asked if I could foster
her for a month. I'm afraid that will not now be
possible. She's barely been here five days and I find
myself counting the hours till she leaves. You see,
I—

Makena slammed the laptop shut. Blood roared in her ears. It had all been a lie. Everything. The entire time she'd been in Scotland Helen had only been pretending to care while counting the hours until Makena, a 'terrible mistake', was sent away again.

The previous day they'd had so fun much baking, visiting Glencoe and reading *The Velveteen Rabbit* that Makena had caught herself wishing she could stay for ever in this magical mountain hideaway. She'd wondered if Helen felt the same way.

She'd even warmed to Ray, reasoning that any man who'd risk his life to play with foxes in the snow was probably ninety-five per cent good. They shared a secret. She knew that he knew she was taking care of the cubs until he was strong again. Plus he was a mountaineer, a species for which she had the greatest affection and admiration.

But none of that mattered now she knew the

truth. Helen didn't want her. Had, in fact, been so desperate to get rid of her that she'd written to the adoption agency on Christmas Eve. Doubtless, she was planning to break the news to Makena as soon as Christmas was over.

Makena was devastated. She'd been a fool to believe there'd be any other outcome. In Nairobi, the other orphans had been glad for her but had warned her not to get her hopes up. They'd told her that few twelve-year-olds were adopted because foster parents preferred babies and toddlers, and that even if Helen did take her on it might not work out.

'People are different when they're in their own country. Maybe she'll be a terrible cook or have a bad temper. Maybe you won't fit in there. Maybe the other villagers will be racist and tell you to go home to Africa.'

Makena glanced at the clock. It would be light soon. She grabbed a banana and two mince pies and swallowed a glass of water. Where she was going, she'd need all the strength she could get.

THE RULES OF
MOUNTAINEERING

- Always triple-check the weather and ensure you have the correct equipment, clothing and supplies before heading out. Take a fully charged phone

- Do all you can to minimise risk. Don't be a hero

- Listen to your body and mind

Makena's father had drummed these rules into her from an early age, and yet she'd escaped The Great Escape without thinking about any of them. All her backpack contained was an extra sweater, one bottle of water, Snow's jar of melted snow

(now freezing again), and the photos of her parents, removed from their frames. The banana and the mince pies had long since been devoured.

Starting out, she'd been quite pleased with her decision. The day had dawned fine and bright and she'd made rapid progress up the mountain. Her plan had been to head for the pass. She recalled seeing a petrol station about two kilometres beyond it. If she made it that far, she might be able to sneak aboard a lorry to Inverness or Edinburgh. What she'd do once she got there, she wasn't sure. She'd come up with some ideas along the way.

But the weather had turned from sunny to stormy with disconcerting speed. Fast-moving clouds had gobbled the summit. Mist oozed from the crevices and gullies, and a bitter wind seemed intent on hurling her into space.

Makena knew from her father's stories that fog was as deadly to climbers as any avalanche. Lose your bearings on a mountain and a hundred hazards lie in wait. From the ground, she'd been able to see a clear route up the mountain. Higher up, it was more difficult. The path kept merging with sheep trails. Rock falls confused things further. Twice she had to take detours around snowdrifts. When the path forked she had to use her best guess.

Now it split again. Makena went left. After battling uphill and sideways for another ten minutes, the trail ended at a frozen waterfall.

Trying not to panic, she retraced her steps. The path fizzled out. When she found another, it soon split into three.

Makena stopped to catch her breath. She had Elvis legs. That's what climbers called it when their thighs and calves wouldn't stop trembling. Her feet were rubbed raw and she had a raging thirst. Earlier, she'd seen the lights blink on in the faraway cottage.

Imagining Helen waking on Christmas morning to find the girl in her care gone made Makena feel unwell.

Had the police been called? Would Helen regret writing the email or would she, like Uncle Edwin, be relieved that she had a good excuse for dispatching Makena back to Africa if and when she did reappear? But whatever was happening in the valley below was a mystery. Like Makena herself, it was lost in the mist.

It was snowing again. Hard. Makena let out a sob. She was going to die on the mountain and she'd have no one to blame but herself.

Terror threatened to overwhelm her. She fought it off by taking deep gulps of brutally cold air. She had to get a grip, as her father would say. The situation was fixable. She could turn back. Returning to the cottage would be humiliating but she'd be alive. And warm. She would insist that Helen return her to Nairobi on the next available plane.

She chose the path that looked most likely to wind its way downhill. As she rounded a tall, jagged rock, she stopped in fright. The silver fox was in her path. Against the snowy backdrop, it was nearly invisible except for one thing: it glowed.

Up close, it was evident that it was not a white version of a red fox but another species altogether, one with thick, soft fur, a pretty, pointed face and vivid blue eyes that seemed to stare right into her soul.

Once Makena had recovered, she was so relieved to see another living creature that she had to remind herself that it was a wild animal, not a sweet ginger cub like those in the shed. It could attack her. Still, its presence gave her a boost. As nightmarish as the situation was, at least she wasn't alone.

Then the fox moved and she screamed. Not because she was afraid it was going to bite her but because she saw, through the swirling white, the cliff

edge that lay beyond it. If it hadn't blocked her way, she'd have fallen.

Staggered at how close she'd come to disaster, she turned to see the fox's ghostly outline melting into the gloom. Makena scrambled after it. It had saved her life once and might do so again. If it was accustomed to getting treats from Ray it might lead her down the mountain to the cottage.

The fox followed a twisting trail visible only to itself. Sometimes it trotted so quickly and surely that Makena struggled to keep up. At other times it seemed to go in circles. She never lost faith that it knew where it was going nor that it wanted her to follow. Its shimmering tail shone through the blizzard like a guiding star.

She was near to collapse when a shepherd's hut loomed out of the storm. Makena halted, breath steaming from her lungs in white puffs. Afraid that it might be a mirage, she took a hesitant step towards it. It seemed solid enough.

Helen had explained that, across the Highlands, there were bothies – basic shelters that could be used for refuge by hikers and climbers. They were free to anyone who needed them.

Makena broke into a tired run. The steps were piled with snow and the door so aged and swollen with moisture that at first she was convinced it was locked. Finally, it creaked open. Only when she stepped over the threshold did she glance back. The shining fox was gone.

THE BOY WHO LIVED
WITH FISHES

Inside the bothy she found water and a kettle. There was no firewood but she did find plenty of bedding and a solar lamp. She set the lamp on the window ledge and its bloom of yellow brought a homely light to the freezing bothy. With bloodless fingers, she struggled to make herself a cup of tea. She was shaking so hard she kept spilling it. Everything hurt, her heart most of all.

Outside, the storm was intensifying. Was it her imagination or was the wind calling her name? Wrapped in a duvet and three blankets, she huddled in a dilapidated armchair. Her eyelids drooped. She wanted to sleep, but knew that if she had hypothermia there was a real chance she might never wake up.

Then again, would that be such a terrible thing?

If she could rewind the clock, she'd go back to Christmas Eve when she and Helen were making mince pies in the warm kitchen, laughing at the ones that went wrong. She'd spent almost the whole day smiling.

Now it was over. She'd burned her bridges. She had no home and no family. She was unloved. Unwanted.

Her eyes slid shut.

Then they snapped open. No, she refused to give up. Snow would never have let go of life. If one breath of air had remained in her lungs, she would use it to dance and convince everyone around her to do the same. That's what made Makena so sure that her best friend was alive and only missing.

'*Climbing is like life,*' her father had said. '*You start slowly. You try one way and if it doesn't work out or you meet some obstacles, you keep searching until you find another trail. There is always a second chance.*'

Makena had tried numerous trails and she'd had second chances and third, fourth and tenth ones. She'd also given plenty of chances to others. And yet here she was, stuck in a stone bothy in a country far from her own.

But if she used Snow's magic moment principle, things were far from hopeless. On Christmas Eve she'd had more magic moments than she could count, and today, one of the worst days of her life, she'd already had five.

I) She'd woken safe and warm in a cloud-soft bed, two things she'd have given her right arm for in Mathare Valley. That counted as at least one magic moment. 2) The fox cubs had fallen upon her with squeals of appreciation and joy when she'd gone to the shed to feed them. 3) The sun had shown up and bathed the snowy mountains in peach light as she set out on her journey. 4) The silver fox had stopped her from plunging to her death. 5) It had led her to shelter.

So although the outlook was bleak, five special things had happened and she was only halfway through Christmas Day.

How could she give up on life when there were mountains to climb and books to read? Some mountains would be friendlier than others, and some would be downright hostile, but she wanted to climb them anyway or rescue people who got into trouble climbing them (like her).

The fox hadn't saved her by accident. It had saved her for a reason. Helen had done the same thing. If she'd later changed her mind, then it was up to Makena to convince her she was wrong. First, though, she had to survive until she was found. That could be days.

Makena couldn't get warm. Shivers ran through her as if she'd taken a dip in a Highland stream. She was well aware that she should get up, make more tea and do star jumps to get the blood pumping through her veins, but she'd done that once and it hadn't helped. She was drowsy.

All ... she ... wanted ... was ... to ... s-l-e-e-p.

'No!' Makena slapped her own cheeks and pummelled her arms. She had to stay awake.

A memory came rushing back. She and her mother sitting on the banks of the dam at the rose farm. Makena had pleaded again for Mama to tell the story of her mysterious childhood friend, Lucas, the boy who'd 'lived among fishes'. To her surprise, her mother relented.

The tale began with them growing up in South Africa, where Betty's father had worked for ten years as headmaster of a school in Maputo. They were inseparable. Among other things, they shared a passion for physics.

'Lucas was brilliant – almost a prodigy.'

'But you're brilliant, Mama.'

'Not like he was. He was the type of boy you just knew would change the world.'

'And did he?'

'Depends on your point of view. One day he didn't turn up at school. I went to his house and he and his family had disappeared. Nobody knew where. It was as if they'd been beamed up to space by aliens.'

'I thought you didn't believe in aliens.'

'Do you want to hear the story or not?'

Makena nodded eagerly.

'The loss of Lucas left a huge hole in my life. I was haunted by the not knowing. Why? Where? How? It was two years before I saw him again, in the last place I could ever have imagined – at a healing ceremony performed by a famous traditional healer, a *sangoma*, from South Africa. Now you know me. I love tradition but have little time for superstition. Even as a teenager, I considered myself a scientist through and through. But I have the greatest respect for those *sangomas* who use their gifts and skills to help others. Their knowledge of illness and disease and of the healing powers of plants can equal, and even far exceed, that of Western doctors.'

'Did you talk to Lucas? What had he been doing?'

Her mama refused to be hurried. 'He was sitting apart from everyone in the shadows. I'd have missed him except that he had a habit of pushing his glasses up his nose. I noticed someone do that and

I hesitated. He jumped up and ran to me. We both wept.'

'Did you ask him why he never said goodbye? Why was he there? Was he sick?'

Betty took a moment to compose herself. 'He was the *sangoma*'s apprentice.'

Whatever Makena was expecting it wasn't that. 'What happened to physics and studying the universe?'

'The ones who came to tell him he'd been chosen to assist the *sangoma* were not interested in his career. They thought they were doing him a great honour. All he had to do was agree and he and his family would never want for anything ever again. Lucas's parents were desperately poor. He did what he thought best for them and his sisters. Besides, he was flattered that the *sangoma* considered him so special. He wasn't to know that the first challenge of his apprenticeship would be to spend six months underwater with fishes.'

Makena was wide-eyed. 'But that's impossible.'

'That's what I said. But Lucas insisted he'd lived in a cave beneath a lake the entire time. He described it as cold, green and lonely. Before I could question him further, he was called away. I'll never forget his face as we parted. He said: "Betty, I didn't choose this life. All I ever wanted was to be an ordinary schoolboy."'

'Did you believe it, Mama? That he'd lived for six months under the lake?'

'No, but he did. So I had to ask myself why. This was a boy who dealt only in fact. He was incapable of lying. I came to the conclusion that there were three possibilities. Number one: he'd been trained to spend a long time — not months but maybe hours — underwater using reeds to breathe, as the old hunters did. Two: he'd spent six months underwater in a parallel universe.'

Makena laughed, but her mother was serious. 'Many physicists, including Stephen Hawking, are open to the possibility that parallel universes or even multiverses exist. They've never been disproved.'

'And what's the third explanation?'

'That Lucas's heart was broken and he couldn't think straight.'

'But what if it was true?' pressed Makena. 'What if he really did live underwater?'

'Honey, please. You know that's not possible.'

Makena disagreed. 'You told Uncle Samson that everything can be explained by physics in the end and if it can't be explained, it's not the end. So maybe it's not the end. Maybe one day it will be explained.'

Her mama laughed and admitted she had a point. 'It was Einstein's belief that there are only two ways to live your life. One is as though nothing is a miracle. The other is as though everything is a miracle.'

'*I* believe in miracles,' said Makena.

Her mother hugged her. 'And so do I.'

Shivering in the bothy armchair, Makena understood why the story had come back to her. She too had spent six months slipping in and out of parallel universes. She too hadn't asked for it. All she'd ever wanted was to be an ordinary schoolgirl with one or two extraordinary dreams.

Unfortunately, in this universe, ice was chugging through her veins. Her head tipped forward. Sleep swooped down.

♥

'Makena! MAKENA!'

The door flew open. Ray stood swaying in the light of his torch, more snowman than human. He rushed to her and lifted her into his arms. His cheeks were wet and she couldn't tell if it was because the icicles in his hair were melting. When he spoke, his voice was deep and strong, the voice of a man half his age.

'Makena, sweet child, oh, thank goodness you're alive. I'm sorry it took me so long to find you. If it hadn't been for the fox ... Makena, Helen is in pieces. She needs you. We both need you, hen. If it's all right, I've come to take you home.'

THE FOX ANGEL

'The secret to toasting marshmallows is to hold them over the embers and twist for about thirty seconds,' said Helen. She and Makena were sitting side by side in front of the fire, forks outstretched. 'Timing is everything. Too close to the flames and they're burned to a crisp. But with patience and a touch of daring, this is the result: honeycomb-brown on the outside, gooey in the middle. How's that? Any good?'

Mouth full, Makena nodded approval. It was Christmas night. Toasted coconut marshmallows were the final item on the menu of Helen's long-delayed Christmas feast. Makena could barely fit them in but they were worth the effort.

'Nothing quite like a stroll on the mountain in a wee blizzard to make you appreciate the simple things in life,' commented Ray, who was sitting on the sofa putting the finishing touches to a wood carving. 'Show me the man who thinks that a posh London restaurant can produce anything superior to a toasted marshmallow and I'll show him.'

He glanced over at Makena, who was twirling a marshmallow as instructed. When it was just the right side of crispy, squishy and burned, she popped it into her mouth. Her eyes squeezed shut in ecstasy. 'My face right now?' she suggested, opening them again.

Ray grinned. 'As I was saying, the simple things beat the finer things every time.'

To Makena, the events of the day had taken on a surreal quality, especially the part where she'd been put on a stretcher and flown over the snowy mountains in an orange helicopter. Ray had summoned it soon after finding her. It had swooped in out of the storm, blades thumping, and plucked them both to safety. Within the hour, Makena had been thawing out in a hot bath.

It would be a while before she stopped feeling guilty for causing so many people so much anguish. She'd tried to apologise to the rescue pilot for dragging him out on Christmas Day, but he wouldn't hear of it.

'*Ach*, away with you. It's nae bother. This is what I signed up for – something more thrilling than Agatha Christie on the telly. Besides, you've returned the favour already. I've been spared lunch with the mother-in-law.'

Seeing Helen again had been a lot harder.

'As long as I live, I don't ever want to feel this way again,' she'd told Makena after they'd had a good cry and a cuddle. 'When I saw your empty bed and footsteps in the snow, I thought I was going to have a heart attack on the spot.'

'I thought you didn't want me. I thought you'd only been pretending to care and that you'd send me away as soon as Christmas was over.'

'Well, now you know that nothing could have been further from my mind,' said Helen. 'I was writing to the adoption agency to ask if you could stay longer. As soon as you stepped off the plane, all I could think was how silly I'd been to suggest fostering you for four short weeks. I knew right then that I wanted you to stay for a lifetime.

'I was determined to give you a perfect Scottish Christmas in the hope that I could convince you — and the authorities, of course — to allow me to adopt you, but everything kept going wrong. Your flight was delayed, I nearly scalded you with hot chocolate, then the weather was foul, then Dad fell ill and … oh, you know the rest.'

Makena was sheepish. 'Yes, I do. I read an email that was private, got the wrong idea, ran away, nearly fell over a cliff, got hypothermia and ruined everyone's Christmas.'

Helen laughed. 'That's a version of events, but it won't be the one I remember. Makena, don't you understand what a blessing you've been? I have a chance of adopting the daughter I've always dreamed of. More than that, you've given me back my dad. Whatever the challenges going forward, this will always be the best Christmas of my life. Which reminds me …'

She stood and went over to the mantelpiece. She handed Makena a purple envelope. 'DO NOT OPEN UNTIL CHRISTMAS DAY! THAT'S AN

ORDER!' was scrawled across the top in silver ink.

Makena stared at the postmark. 'I don't know anyone in Chicago.'

Helen smiled. 'Why don't you open it and find out who it's from?'

As soon as Makena saw the poppy card inside, she knew.

Happy Kissmass, Kissmass!
My new mom wanted me to spell it properly but I said it had to be this way. You'd understand.

They tell me you're in Scotland. You can probably fill a jar or two with snow over there. I could fill a few million here in Chicago. Everyone here calls me Diana because there's so much actual snow it got confusing. That's

317

cool with me. After all, I am named after the
Queen of the Supremes.

You probably want to know how I fell off the
earth. I thought the same about you. You're
getting the short version because I can't fit
much on the card.

Remember me telling you that life sometimes
springs a nasty surprise, and that's why we get
at least three magic moments every day — to
make up for it? Well, it's all true.

I don't remember the part where the bulldozer
ran over me. When I finally woke up in hospital,
I didn't know my own name. They said it
was amnesia caused by shock. The doctors
and nurses were all depressed-looking and

they started going on about my future in a wheelchair. I told them to put that thought in the rubbish bin where it belonged because this girl is going to dance and have her name in lights like Michaela DePrince. Funny, I didn't remember much but I remembered Michaela and you.

You're wondering where the magic moment is, aren't you? I went on about Michaela so much that word got to a surgeon who volunteers for a charity that works in war zones. He'd seen her dance with the Dance Theatre of Harlem. Long story short, he operated on me for free. It helped a lot. I also got glasses. Who knew that words and pictures could be so clear?! Eventually, my memory came back and I got adopted by an African American

319

family. They're the best. I'm their third and last (maybe) adopted kid. The others are from Japan and Burundi. My new sister, May, says that the twenty-second Emperor of Japan was an albino!

'Course, life is no fairy tale, so I'm a little way from joining the Dutch National Ballet, like Michaela. About three operations and a decade of practice away. Meanwhile, I've started ballet classes. I sit in my chair and watch but I'm plotting the moves for when it's my time.

Sorry I didn't get you a Christmas present. You gave me one and you didn't even know it! I used to have three magic moments every day. Now I'm guaranteed four. Sunrise, sunset and

a random one. The fourth moment is a memory.
You and me dancing Slum Lake while Innocent
and his crew played their hearts out. We nailed
it, girl, didn't we?

Keep dancing and climbing those mountains.

Love,
Diana (Snow to you) xx
Your best friend (I hope!) xx

The words blurred before Makena's eyes. She was
incapable of speech. Helen did it for her.

'Friendships like yours and Snow's, they're for
life. I'll do everything in my power to see that the two
of you are reunited soon. The same goes for Africa.
It'll always be home to both of us. Whether we're in
Scotland, thinking about ways to help Hearts4Africa,

or in Nairobi with Edna at the Home for Girls, you'll always be connected to your country. But in time I hope you come to love Scotland too.'

Makena speared another marshmallow and looked over at Ray. She couldn't get over the change in him. Neither could Dr Brodie.

'If Ray were an ordinary mortal, a mountain rescue operation in a blizzard so soon after near-pneumonia would have killed him,' he'd told Makena when he came to check her over. 'Ironically, it seems to have been the exact tonic he needed. Makena, you've reminded him of his purpose in life – to help people and teach them to enjoy the mountains safely. He's a man reborn.'

They'd done a great deal of talking, Makena and Ray. Helen was right. They did have a lot in common.

But the subject to which they kept returning was the silver fox.

When it came flying out of the snowstorm like a silver bullet, yelping at him to follow it, he'd doubted the evidence of his own eyes. In all his years in the mountains, he'd never seen an Arctic fox. 'We don't have silver foxes in the wild in Scotland, Makena, only red ones. If I'd encountered one before I'd have remembered, I can assure you.'

'So the night I saw an Arctic fox standing beside you in the garden, you had no clue it was there?'

Ray shook his head. 'I did not. I do recall a powerful sense of peace coming over me as I looked up at the mountain. In all honesty, I hadn't felt that way since before I lost my wife. I stayed longer than I should have because I didn't want to break the spell. But no, I didn't see any silver fox – not that night and not until it appeared out of the blizzard.'

'What do you think it was, then, the fox on the mountain?' persisted Makena. 'An escaped Arctic fox that's super-smart and likes saving humans who like saving animals? Or was it a ghost? Or maybe an angel?'

'Perhaps it was a combination of all three,' suggested Helen. 'Maybe it was everything and everyone you've ever loved made manifest in one perfect fox.'

'Could be,' agreed Ray. He leaned forward and handed Makena the finished carving. 'A present for you, hen. Better late than never. Happy Christmas.'

It was a fox with tiny wings. Every feather and every whisker was perfectly sculpted in walnut wood. Makena stroked it. 'A fox angel! Oh, it's beautiful. Is it really for me?'

'Absolutely. No one else I know appreciates foxes quite as much as you and I do.'

Makena pressed it to her cheek. The wood was still warm from his workings. 'Thanks, Ray. It's going on my bedside table next to my precious things – my mama and baba's photos and my Snow jar.'

'I'm delighted you like it so much, hen. Believe it or not, I started carving it before I saw the fox on the mountain, after I spotted you sneaking out in the midnight garden to feed the cubs. I wanted to thank you. I knew at once that we were kindred spirits.'

'That's one way of putting it,' Helen remarked drily. 'Partners in crime is another. I can see I'm going to have to keep a close eye on you both.'

A rush of happiness filled Makena to bursting. The faces of her mama and baba floated into her mind and she no longer felt guilty. She knew that they would have wanted this for her, wanted her to find a special home and a loving family.

'Mum,' she said shyly, testing out the word, 'would you mind if I put the fox angel at the top of the tree?'

Helen's smile was so wide it could have wrapped around Makena twice. 'Do you know, I can't think of anything I'd like more. Looks to me as if it belongs there.'

'Between every two pine trees there
is a doorway to a new life.'

John Muir

AUTHOR'S NOTE AND ACKNOWLEDGEMENTS

The Snow Angel is, for me, about the world's forgotten children. It's also about the power of love and nature to heal the broken-hearted, and about the ties that bind us all.

Some books have a definite beginning. For instance, the idea for *The White Giraffe* came to me when I was walking down a London street one December, on my way to do some Christmas shopping. Out of nowhere, an image of a girl riding a giraffe popped into my head. Growing up on a farm and game reserve in Zimbabwe, I actually had a pet giraffe called Jenny and I thought: Wouldn't it be the coolest thing in the world if you could ride a giraffe?

In some ways, the story behind *The Snow Angel* has been unfolding all my life. The landscape, culture and magic in the novel are based on my experiences, both beautiful and harrowing, as a child in Zimbabwe, and on decades of adult journeys through South Africa, Kenya, Namibia, Malawi and Mozambique.

The journeys of Makena and Snow mostly had their genesis in the events of the last few years. As the antics of celebrities and random cruelties of politicians dominated the headlines, I became increasingly frustrated that the struggles of the most vulnerable people and wild animals on our earth often went unmentioned.

When the 2014 Ebola crisis began in Guinea and Sierra Leone, there was a great deal of panic in countries such as the UK about what might happen if the virus reached our shores. Then when a trial vaccine proved effective in late 2016, there was an international sigh of relief. When a fresh Ebola outbreak was reported in the Democratic Republic of Congo in May 2017, little attention was paid to it.

What hasn't, and won't go away, are the Ebola orphans, whose pain is compounded if they're later rejected by their communities on superstitious grounds. In one heartbreaking case, a girl who'd lost sixteen family members was unable to return to her home village because some believed she was a witch.

The plight of children with albinism is also devastating. In some countries – Tanzania and Malawi are just two of them – the only safe place for them is in guarded institutions, so valuable are they to those who believe their body parts can bring power, wealth or good fortune. One would imagine that every good and decent leader across the world would be united in wanting to save these children, change local hearts and minds and bring those responsible to justice, but this, too, rarely makes the news.

In Zimbabwe alone, there are over a million orphans. Within a 10km radius of Harare, the capital city, there are said to be 60,000 child-headed households. Think about that. In a country where more than 85 per cent of people are unemployed and where there is a cash crisis, 60,000 children are trying to raise other children.

But it was not only these lost and forgotten children who moved me to write *The Snow Angel*. It was also a road trip through the Scottish Highlands with Jules Owen and a midnight encounter with a fox. And, over the years, it was witnessing time after time, how kind hearts change lives.

One story that particularly impacted me was that of Michaela DePrince. A war-child from Sierra Leone, Michaela was adopted by an extraordinary American family. Through their love and her own immense drive, talent and courage, Michaela realised her dream of becoming a dancer, first for the Dance Theatre of Harlem in the US and in recent years for the Dutch National Ballet. Daily, she inspires children across the world.

A large cast of people advised, corrected, rescued or influenced me when I was researching the Kenyan section of the book. Chief among them was CNN correspondent Robyn Kriel, who reported on then US President Barack Obama's 2015 visit to Kenya, and who was at the time of writing based in Nairobi.

Robyn's compassionate reporting on Mathare Valley and passionate reporting on Kenyan success stories was beyond helpful, but it was much more than that. She gave so generously of her time and experience that thanks seems entirely inadequate.

It was Robyn's report on Tambuzi that led me to contact Maggie Hobbs, who warmly and good-humouredly gave me a Skype tour of her famous rose farm.

It's a dream of mine to climb Point Lenana on Mount Kenya. That day might be some way off so until then I relied heavily on the guides and mountaineers who know it best. I am particularly indebted to Simon Gitau, Guardian of Mount Kenya, whose vivid, powerful account of the mountain he loves brought it to life for me. Makena and Baba take the route Simon recommended to Lakes Rutundu and Alice and beyond.

For the mountaineering sections of the book, I'm also thankful to Mount Kenya Climbing Tours and to my amazing, humble friend, Rebecca Stephens MBE, who has not only climbed the Ice Window Route on Mount Kenya but, in 1993, became the first British woman to climb Mount Everest.

I'm deeply grateful to James Macharia and Anne Kinyota as well as to CNN producer Idris Muktar, who grew up in Mathare, for taking the time to read my novel and set me straight on crucial details regarding Kenyan culture, language and geography. Special thanks also to my friend Emelia Sithole-Matarise for being endlessly supportive, patient and encouraging over many coffees and far too many cakes. Any errors in the book are mine and mine alone.

I've heard tales of Tokoloshe encounters all my life in Zimbabwe, but the essence of Lucas's story was drawn from conversations with local guides in Zimbabwe's Honde Valley while on a road trip with my sister, Lisa, and in the Matobo Hills while on a road trip with my dad. A coffee (another one!) with lovely Georgina Godwin in London and a newspaper article on apprentice *sangomas* in South Africa also resonated with me.

I feel it's important to stress that while the slums of Nairobi exist, they are only one aspect of the vibrant, successful and stunningly beautiful country that is Kenya. The same is true of Africa in general. I'm thankful every day to have grown up on a continent so rich in intelligent, creative, generous and big-hearted people.

For keeping the faith for over thirteen years, and for believing in Makena and Snow from the first day they met them, there are no words to express how grateful I am to Fiona Kennedy, my editor and publisher at Zephyr, and to my literary agent, Catherine Clarke. Not only are they both brilliant in every way, they're also two of the best, most wonderful people I've ever known.

Huge thanks also to Catherine Hyde, whose stunning artwork has so perfectly captured what I hope is the spirit of my novel.

Thanks to the dedicated and super-talented team at Head of Zeus, especially Amanda Ridout, Jessie Price, Dan Groenewald, Jon Small, Claire Kennedy, Chrissy Ryan, Jennifer Edgecombe, Kaz Harrison, Suzanne Sangster, Lauren Atherton, Ian Macbeth and Victoria Reed. Copyeditor, Jenny Glencross, and Sue Michniewicz, who designed the glorious interior of the novel, were also invaluable.

Lastly, a big thanks to my mom, an ace research assistant and my biggest supporter.

When I do school visits and speak at festivals, children often ask how they can make a difference in the world. With all that's going on, it can be easy to feel overwhelmed. But if each and every one of us did one kind thing every week or, better still, every day, imagine the difference we could make. So here are some suggestions:

- ♥ Open your heart to refugees and migrants. Few choose to leave their homes. Like Makena, they've had the lives they've built stolen from them by disease, drought, war, unemployment or other circumstances beyond their control. Most bring knowledge, experience or gifts that enrich our own communities. In *The Snow Angel*, Makena repays Helen for helping to rescue her by healing and bringing joy to Helen and Ray. It's an exchange.

- ♥ Say no to the plastic bags, ear buds and straws that pollute our oceans.

- ♥ Adopt animals from shelters. Don't give money to pet shops and puppy farms. I adopted my Bengal, Max, from the RSPCA and he has repaid me with unconditional love a thousand times over.

- ♥ Consider becoming a vegetarian or vegan.

- ♥ If you love books, support or fight to save your local library. You might be lucky enough to have books at home or school. Millions don't.

♥ Speak out against cruelty. Stand up against injustice.

♥ Plant a tree or flowers that help save bees.

♥ Sponsor a child or animal. As an Ambassador for the Born Free Foundation (www.bornfree.org.uk), I can whole-heartedly say that their work with wildlife and local communities in Kenya and beyond is worth your time and/ or donation. Lewa Wildlife Conservancy (www.lewa.org) also does incredible work with children and animals in the Mount Kenya region. In the UK, Goodheart helps suffering farm animals (www.goodheartanimalsanctuaries.com).

♥ The truth matters. So does respect. Hold fast to both.

♥ Be kind. It costs nothing and it might just save a life.

Lauren St John
London ♥
2017